VENOM

JOHN LEE SCHNEIDER

'If a black mamba should so much as scratch you with one of its fangs, it's going to kill you.'
Donald Strydom
Black Mamba! (2002)

SEVEREDPRESS

VENOM

WWW.SEVEREDPRESS.COM

ISBN: 978-1-923165-47-2

CHAPTER 1

Jack was looking for a black mamba.

The brush in the little wooded area was heavy. He would have to be extremely careful. Mambas didn't allow second chances.

Dendroaspis polylepis – they called it the '*seven-step snake*', because after being bitten, you only took seven steps before you dropped dead.

As his college herp-professor told him, “If you get bit, that's all you get.”

That was an exaggeration, of course, but depending upon the severity of envenomation, not by very damn much. A black mamba had the fastest-acting toxin known among venomous snakes, so symptoms could take-over in a hurry. Jack remembered a case where a man was found sitting in a boat, with a venom-kit in his lap – cause of death, a mamba-bite, presumably taken from an overhanging tree-branch as he traversed the river, and it paralyzed him before he could give himself a shot.

Most likely, that was a case of direct arterial envenomation, high-balling the neurotoxin effects, which shut down breathing, resulting in cardiovascular-failure.

But even in average cases, bite-victims reported feeling symptoms almost immediately, becoming debilitating within ten to twenty minutes. After that, it was just a matter of how fast it took you over. Untreated, it typically took no more than four hours to finally die.

And before the introduction of antivenin, death was nearly certain. There were few things as close to a hundred-percent as the fatality-rate for the bite of a black mamba. And while there were always exceptions, because, in the end, a sufficient dose of toxin has to enter the system, the fact was, mamba venom was so virulent, that even the slightest amount introduced into the bloodstream was *always* enough to cause respiratory distress, and therefore, always enough to kill.

There was also the abiding fact that mambas had no 'dry-bite'. And while, there were the isolated cases of people taking nips from black mambas and reporting no symptoms, these were mostly cases of slashing bites, where the venom is released outside the wound. There was also one specific case, recorded on camera, involving a captive mamba, where a bite bled profusely, flushing out the venom.

But such cases were the medical equivalent of falling out of a plane and landing in a random pile of hay. It *happened* but, it wasn't the way to bet.

Black mambas were native to sub-Saharan Africa. Generally, they were considered rare in northwest Oregon's temperate Willamette Valley.

But right now, Jack was looking for two of them. The female was gravid – pregnant – about to lay eggs.

And if only that were the worst of it, because there were a lot more than just a pair of mambas out there.

Jack guessed that, within the surrounding three-to-five square miles, were enough highly-venomous animals, dose-for-dose, to kill every single person in all the adjoining suburban neighborhoods.

Just by itself, a single mamba contained enough venom to kill ten men in a single bite.

Jack worked running '*Venom Lab*', a snake-milking and breeding operation, run as part of the toxicology-department of the local med-school. They had a building off the main-campus, twenty-miles west, in the bedroom suburb town of Silver Lake. It carried the deliberately innocuous title, '*Willamette Institute*', and it sat off a main through-way, bordering the residential neighborhoods where Highway 26 split the suburbs from the wooded areas and farmlands on its way to the coast. The location was chosen for zoning reasons, because the Institute originally started as an animal-research lab, with live animals on-site – something that had long drawn the ire of the local activist community.

In point of fact, the vivisectionist-stuff mostly didn't happen there. Jack was aware of very little knife-work. Most of it was drug research. That actually dovetailed nicely with Jack's own department, which, for safety's sake, was kept carefully sequestered on the other side of the building.

The Venom Lab housed some of the deadliest animals on Earth. There were not just snakes, but spiders, scorpions – those pale, scampering Death-stalkers – not to mention giant hornets. And damn-near *all* of them had been released into the surrounding neighborhoods.

Jack shut his eyes, painfully remembering the news-coverage that day.

The Institute was already under fire for the vivisectionist-stuff and the local press had a tendency to simply repeat accusations from protesters, with only cursory follow-up from the facility itself. Even then, it was mostly stock interview footage from the med-school's administrative head, Dean Herman Brown. Less often, it was from Jack's own immediate superior, Doctor Janice McCoy, who oversaw the animal-research center building itself.

In point of fact, the Institute was already in the process of shutting down.

Recent events, both involving harassment and sabotage, had convinced the higher-ups – that is to say, the investors who pulled the money-strings – that the local region had simply become too toxic. The Venom

Lab was being moved to Idaho, an effort to keep the facility semi-localized geographically. Jack planned to move with it.

Unfortunately, the situation had escalated. Because now there were a few dead people involved, and one of them was a student at the university, a popular young woman who also happened to be the daughter of one of those same investors.

The news was still coming out about *that* little tidbit.

So now, on top of false reports about what happened to the cats, dogs, and monkeys on the other side of the building, people were apparently shocked to discover they had a venom-farm in their midst. It'd only been public knowledge for ten years.

From Jack's view, he actually thought a little fear of the place couldn't hurt, because the harassment and vandalism was growing bolder. Recently, it finally started becoming dangerous.

Jack had two interns, grad-students, under his direct supervision, Lindsey and Chuck, and both had been subject to catcalls and intimidation – and in Chuck's case, actual assault.

Chuck was just a little guy, too. He always emphasized that he liked to be called '*Charles*', and apparently just to bother him, everybody, Jack included, always insisted on '*Chuck*'. He *really* hated '*Chuckie*'.

He was the type known to pick up spiders in a cup and carry them outside. Jack, who had once been beaten-up by the football-team over a girl, described him as the sort of a guy you could understand why he got punched a lot. Chuck was a bit little-brotherly.

As if to affirm, he once told Jack he'd been that way since he was a kid. "My big brother used to take after me something awful. His friends too."

Jack, whose own older brother was a master of such draconian torments as noogies, wedgies, monkey-bumps,

Dutch-rubs, on top of simple generalized beatings, supposed he could sympathize there.

On this particular day, however, it was Chuck's badge from the Institute that got him targeted.

He and Jack were both standing at the public-transit, light-rail station, when someone with one of those long wooden skateboards came darting by and whacked him across the back of the head with the board.

Jack's own badge was under his jacket, or it might have been him. Chuck was knocked unconscious.

The assailant hopped back on his skateboard, laughing, actually mugging the surrounding security cameras, before Jack stepped forward and slugged him in the face, clothes-lining him off the board, and planting him hard on his back.

Jack hovered threateningly over the guy with a raised fist.

"I'm *seventeen*," the young hooligan was wailing, rolling on the ground, holding his face. "You can't *hit* me."

Just for that, Jack slugged him twice more. The kid was still down when the transit police appeared on the scene – arresting Jack, and sending both Chuck and his underage assailant to the hospital.

There had actually been talk of charges. The kid's name was Addy Robins, and his mother was a local schoolteacher – apparently the type *Pink Floyd* wrote songs about. Despite seventeen-year-old Addy having just committed criminal assault, and Jack having administered nothing other than a few facial bruises, Mrs. Robins made an attempt to press criminally.

Unfortunately for young Addy, his mugging the security camera, after nearly cracking Chuck's skull, didn't play as well for the D.A. as it did for the local news, and their case was promptly turned away. Jack himself only spent a few hours in jail, although that still provided a mug-shut for the press to run on the evening news every time his name or the Institute came up.

In the aftermath of the incident, the university, in the person of Dean Herman Brown, formally petitioned the city to beef-up security around the place, and young Addy had been issued a restraining order.

Addy, however, was just one of the foot-soldiers. The problem was really a community full of Addys. Because in a few years, this kid would grow into a bigger problem, and there were already lots of those all over the city.

A man named James Warden – 'The Warden', as he liked to be called – was currently the primary local example. He was a typical Oregon militant. A guy from out of state, who liked to start fires under the banner of a cause. Exultant destruction, they called it.

'The Warden' had followers nationwide, and could be counted on to draw at least a parking lot's worth of demonstrators, in any given state, guided simply by his posts on social-media – basically, flash-mob protests on-demand.

According to James Warden's website, they targeted the '*unmoved and unrepentant*'. That meant the courts had the temerity to support some corporation, business – or Institute's – right to exist. Therefore, the Warden and his group would simply take matters into their own hands.

And as demonstrated by the attack on Chuck, that simply meant activating local-cells of wayward kids, who needed direction, and reapply their street-thuggery to the cause.

If ya wanna clobber someone, make sure it's someone wearing *this* badge. Wanna start a fire? Go for it – just make sure the building has *this* logo.

Then all that antisocial acting-out became a *good* thing. In the absence of actual leaders, it was '*give them* causes *to follow and enemies to hate*'.

It was really a matter of tapping into that segment of the population who was always ever-ready to burn down Frankenstein's Castle and redirecting them where to point their pitchforks and torches.

Or skateboards.

Chuck had turned his head at the last second, or that board would have caught him with its edge instead of the flat, in which case, it might have split his skull rather than just knocked him out.

Jack had always taken public transit. It was PC for the university, but they simply couldn't do it anymore.

That, at least, wasn't a problem for his other intern. Lindsey had herself a nice old-fashioned gas-guzzling sixties Mustang.

Lindsey was a fight waiting to happen for another reason. It wasn't her fault – she just looked *that* good.

Chuck, who always managed to get his face in the way, had taken a couple of punches on her account too, although that instance just got him a couple pairs of regular old knuckles, and hadn't required a hospital visit.

Lindsey was twenty-three and a grad-student. She stood with the physical poise of a gymnast, and was attractive enough that Jack, himself, had taken a good deal of ribbing from his colleagues, suggesting *that* was the reason she was there.

In point of fact, his own direct superior, the aforementioned Dr. Janice McCoy, was one.

Janice was second at the university, after Dean Brown, although she ceded expertise in the Venom Lab to Jack.

He had known her, mostly amicably, for nearly twenty-years, ever since his first year at the state university.

Of course, both of them consciously never mentioned they'd had a beer-soaked one-nighter in Jack's dorm-room, after a fraternity kegger. He was the Freshman, who actually *liked* her. She was the Sophomore, who was embarrassed about it the next day, and hoping her football-playing boyfriend wouldn't find out.

That was not helped when Jack's roommate bugled the news of their drunken tryst to anyone within earshot, accompanied by Janice' new nickname, '*Jump Your Bones McCoy*'.

It was a name, unfortunately, that stuck.

Janice' boyfriend, a popular quarterback, enjoying his senior year before the pros, hadn't much liked it. He and several members of the starting lineup met Jack walking home one night, along a wooded stretch between campus buildings, bordering a local cemetery, and they beat him up pretty good.

That was where Jack could relate to Chuck. As a bookish-sort himself all through high school, Jack was never short on posturing meat-heads wanting to take a punch at him. In response, he joined the wrestling team. He also learned karate and boxing.

None of which mattered a hoot when Janice' quarterback stepped out of hiding and sucker-punched him. Then five or six guys – Jack never got a clear count – pounded on him for a good solid five-minutes. They were all in the two-thirty-plus pound-range, and after the first punch put Jack down, it was mostly about getting kicked on the ground. In the end, they were actually fairly restrained – nothing was broken, there was no trip to the hospital. After it was over and they all walked away, Jack had crawled to his feet and stumbled home.

Janice and her football-hero split-up shortly thereafter, and she had formally apologized to Jack.

Although, she still held the *Jump Your Bones McCoy* thing against him.

And now she was his boss.

But they mostly got along.

As far as Lindsey went, Jack pushed back firmly on innuendo. In this sort of job, hanky-panky in the office could easily get someone killed.

The fact was, Lindsey was very good – less experienced, but maybe even a better handler than Jack. She was also unique in the trade – she'd never been bitten – not by a snake, not by a lizard. She'd never even been stung by a bee.

She was particularly good with vipers, having grown-up around the variety of rattlers roaming the hills and valleys of southeastern Oregon and northeast California. She also handled cobras well, under supervision, although she expressed less confidence when dealing with some of their Australian elapid relatives, like the tiger or brown snakes, and the taipans made her nervous.

But she was actually a bit phobic about the mambas.

To be fair, that was a good fear to have.

Too bad that group of idiots that broke into the Institute weren't a bit more phobic.

The incident was linked to James Warden, who had just recently been released from a sixty-day stint in jail, a period where most of his local acolytes, of which Addy was only one, continued the relentless harassment and vandalism.

It actually stepped-up, apparently protesting the simple fact of James Warden sitting behind bars at all. Jack, who couldn't take public-transit anymore, now came out the parking lot to find his tires slashed and his windows broken.

Worse, the city, and even the university itself, seemed forgiving of it. Even when individual vandals had been caught, they were usually simply released. Targeted property damage was tolerated so long as you were acting out in the right cause. Vivisection was definitely one – a local buzz-word.

It didn't matter that Jack didn't *do* vivisection work, or that it didn't even go on at the Institute, and never really had – there were statements to be made and flags to be waved, and if Jack was worried about a few six-hundred dollar tires... well, that was just him being petty.

The irony was Jack's animals actually had to be kept in optimum health. He didn't even do his toxicity testing on lab-mice, choosing instead to use human heart-cells, which was a much more accurate barometer of a venom's effect on people.

What Jack did saved thousands of lives every year. And he risked his own every day to do it.

But he was in the same building. And when his car got its tires slashed, the city told him they would 'look into it'.

It didn't even seem to matter that the place was already shutting down. The increased vandalism during James Warden's incarceration, and subsequent release from jail, finally culminated in the break-in two-weeks ago.

And boy, the whole manure-truck hit the fan.

The university was already keeping them at a distance. The vandalism was mostly sequestered at the Institute, and Dean Brown obviously didn't want the med-school itself targeted. And excepting the odd cranium cracked with a skateboard, it had mostly been about property damage.

But once people started ending up dead, that couldn't be brushed aside. Especially when it turned out that one of the deceased was a young woman named Elizabeth Williams, daughter of local businessman, George

Williams, who was one of the university's – and the city's – biggest donors.

Elizabeth, 'Liz', came from the social-work side of the university, focusing on administrative and patient-processing within the medical-field. And the personality drawn to that sort of work was practically painted all over her. A bleeding-heart to the core, she'd been a long-time, vocal critic of the Willamette Institute, and had stood in many protest-lines on the streets outside.

Chuck had also taken a punch on her account once too – actually *by* her, according to Lindsey, who belonged to the same sorority – something about a drunken pass at a freshman-year frat party, and Liz apparently knocked him flat on his butt.

Liz Williams was also a disciple of James Warden and it was suspected she had something to do with getting the security codes that let her and her cohorts into the Institute that night.

The break-in was on camera, catching multiple views of the intruders, all wearing masks. Increment weather earlier in the day had briefly shut down the power, including the security cameras, but they came on in time to clearly catch three individuals in black, walking the hallways past freed monkeys, cats, and dogs, letting them run loose out the propped-open exits.

Then they had moved into the Venom Lab.

What happened next was not clear. Jack was stuck accepting the sheer idiocy of it. You would have thought the danger-signs posted everywhere would allow for a certain amount of caution, cause or no cause, but a fire was somehow started, apparently by accident. The specifics were yet to be determined, but it seemed to be a chemical fire.

Being animal-rights activists, the decision was evidently made that they couldn't let the animals die in their cages and started opening them up.

To say they underestimated the volatility of some of these species would be an understatement.

There had been three intruders, and all three were found dead at the site. The bodies were burned, but the cause of death in each case was snakebite. One was from a cobra. One was a taipan. The last was a mamba bite.

None of the bites were clearly visible on camera, but there was a lot of stumbling and panic in the spreading smoke, as the vandals knocked over half the room-full of surrounding cages full of spiders and scorpions.

Without the flames, most of the escaped critters probably would have simply skittered around the lab until morning. As it was, they fled for the doors like rats swarming off a sinking ship.

Not all of them got out, and a number of them *did* die in the fire, but the flames were actually localized to the Venom Lab itself. Most of it was metal and glass, so it was really only the furniture that burned.

It stormed earlier that day, and the Institute suffered a power failure. The system had still been rebooting, so the sprinklers were slow in response, allowing a certain amount of damage to the lab. The bodies of the vandals were also pretty cooked.

But they were still identifiable. Two of them were local street-kids, who had been in trouble before. And then they identified the third, the mamba-bite victim, as Liz Williams. It was her social-media posts that linked her to James Warden.

Although they had not yet done so, the city was soon expected to be announcing a warrant for Mr. Warden's arrest. James Warden, already freshly out of jail, had so far remained elusive and in hiding.

In the court of public opinion, judgment had yet to be rendered. Liz Williams had been popular at the State University as an undergrad, combining dance-team duties with a student-council campaign. It actually gave her a local fan-following large enough to make half-time news during football games, always accompanied by her leading the dance-squad on the field.

Liz Williams' death was a local shock, especially considering the circumstances, although it really shouldn't have been such a scandal that students would be involved. When Jack himself was in grad-school, he used to joke that universities were stocked with the poster-children for all those old teenage psycho-revenge movies – angry nerds holding a grudge over prom-night.

In this case, the angry nerd seemed to be the prom queen herself.

No doubt due to the influence of her father, the criminal element of the break-in was downplayed in the press, spinning it so that she had 'died doing what she believed.'

All of which was well and good, respectful to the deceased, but it also set the groundwork for the first public calls for an '*investigation*' into her death.

To Jack, that sounded a lot like people with pitch-forks asking directions to Frankenstein's Castle.

Worrisome. But unfortunately, Jack had more pressing concerns, because the damage from the break-in had already been done. Dealing with the aftermath could potentially be a lot worse.

There had been some *real* lethals let loose.

CHAPTER 2

The research building was right at the edge of an open field, north of the highway, with nothing but woods and grassland. And right on the other side was a housing development – right next to a newly-built school.

And why not?

Jack ran a tally in his head. The cast of escapees from the lab was intimidating.

He'd actually already found a number of the spiders and scorpions just outside the Institute. They didn't travel as fast, but they also represented the biggest invasive threat. The temperate environment was not unfavorable, and these were creepy-crawlies you didn't want establishing a breeding population. They had funnel-webs, Brazilian wandering spiders, all kinds of black widows and red-backs. Then, of course, there were those giant hornets. *They* might be anywhere.

There was also no real way to know how many of the 'bugs' actually escaped, versus being burnt in the fire. That might be a problem going forward.

But in the immediate moment, the loose snakes were by far the most pressing danger.

First and foremost, was the specific serpent he was tailing now.

The black mamba was, by Jack's measure, the deadliest snake in the world. Besides its fast-acting, virtual death-sentence of a venom, it was long, slippery, and aggressive. If you unwarily stepped into its striking range, an agitated mamba would have already bitten you twice.

There was a lot of argument in the field over the '*most-dangerous*' snake. In the end, it was about how you measured it.

The most *venomous* snake in terms of smallest-dose required to kill, was Australia's inland taipan, *Oxyuranus microlepidotus.* But it was a small, mild-tempered animal that lived in the middle of a desert-nowhere, never implicated in a single fatality, and only a handful of bites, all successfully treated with antivenin.

Its cousin, on the other hand, the coastal taipan, *O. scutellatus,* with 'only' the third most toxic venom, rivaled the black mamba as Jack's top-pick for 'most dangerous', falling second, only due to its somewhat smaller size and thicker form – stronger, but not as slippery, and easier to handle for a seasoned snake handler, although both species exhibited strong parallel evolution, and were virtual clones of each other.

The real danger from snakebite, however, didn't come from these super-toxic nightmare species. The diminutive saw-scaled viper and puff adders of Africa, along with the Russell's viper and cobras of Asia, killed anywhere from fifty to a hundred-thousand people every year.

These snakes weren't '*seven step*' killers but they were clearly a greater practical *problem* worldwide than, say, a black mamba.

But for Jack, it was about confrontation, no doubt a reflection of his job. His concern was which was more likely to kill you if you stumbled across it. Or in his own case, if you had to deal with it on a daily basis – the one you'd least like loose in the room with you.

On that last point, fair-mention should be made of the reticulated python. Unbothered, a venomous snake most often avoided people. A big retic would sometimes come after you. That was called '*predation*'.

But that took a big constrictor. Some of these hot-herps could kill you right out of the egg, and kill you quickly.

If that gravid female mamba were allowed to lay, she might produce a dozen or more eggs, and then suddenly you had *twelve* one-shot killers.

By their invoice, they were also still missing their coastal taipan, several cobras, including a king.

Cobras were actually easier to deal with than vipers in the field. They were display-oriented. Some of the rattlesnakes were courteous enough to shake a warning, but a cobra got right up and posed.

None of the mambas or their Australian elapid relatives were so accommodating. Taipans tended to present as just a big brown snake until they postured up, not even always flattening into their own elapid-trademarked hood, but simply cocking their heads into that s-pose, and striking.

Jack was at least grateful that none of the lance-head vipers escaped. *They* were mean bastards, known to chase after antagonists. They also had a tendency to roam, as well as being much more acclimated for an environment like the valley. A rain-forest, that supported rattlers in the hills, would certainly be congenial enough for lance-heads.

They were strong snakes too, up to seven-feet of spring-muscle, difficult to wrestle, with *long* viper fangs and an agonizingly painful venom. For Jack's money, they were the worst of the viper-clan, even more than bushmasters or diamondbacks, or even nasty-biters like the hyper-fanged Gaboon adder.

Vipers were a different beast when it came to catching them. They were spring-loaded and lightning fast. Humans simply didn't have the reflective quickness to dodge a strike. On the other hand, they came out of a coil, so evading them was mostly about staying outside their strike range. In that way, they were a bit similar to a reared-up, posturing cobra.

Which, in the end, was why Jack always circled back to the mamba as the worst of the lot. The strike wasn't the spring-loaded viper, but it was lengthwise and straight as an arrow.

It didn't even necessarily have to be an aggressive attack. If you startled a mamba in the bush, especially if it perceived itself cornered, their method of escape was usually to shoot right straight back at you. Jack called it the *bite-and-run*. Mambas were big on that little move. They could streak past you like greased-spaghetti, and hit you twice as they went.

So you had to be careful poking around bushes.

And he knew at least one of the mambas was about. He'd found feces and track-marks.

It was at least three-miles from the Institute, but the little wooded-area, right outside this unsuspecting little neighborhood, was just perfect, with lots of tall grass, as well as a lot of chirping birds and squirrels flitting through the trees and brush – food and shelter.

The little hollow was split by a narrow path, traversed most often by kids on their way to school. Fortunately, it was summer-break.

That provided a finite window for their little round-up.

Not including the 'bugs', the spiders, scorpions, and hornets, for which he had no accurate tally, Jack counted thirty animals that had escaped.

So far, no one had been hurt except for the break-in itself, but news of the mass-escape dovetailed on a lot of already very negative publicity.

On top of the rumors of vivisection, the revelation of the Institute's deadly on-site cast came as a belated shock to the local citizenry, and a number of individuals had not been shy about saying so.

One of these was, of course, Addy's mother, Mrs. Janelle Robins, who was already on a soapbox over Jack's physical handling of her son. She'd been interviewed on the news several times, always with Jack's mugshot broadcast in the corner. She was taking an offensive posture and actually demanding the arrest and prosecution of the Institute's entire staff.

In any other city, Jack wouldn't worry, but it was an election year and local politicians bent like origami to public opinion, usually the loudest and most shrill. That was to say nothing of where the sentiments of donors like George Williams might fall.

Jack gritted his teeth, feeling his frustrated temper threaten.

Standing there alone in the woods, he deliberately stopped for a moment to close his eyes and take a calming breath.

He had to keep his mind on his work. He couldn't let all that distract him, or he could wind up dead very quickly.

When he opened his eyes again, he looked down at his feet and realized he'd just walked up on another track-mark.

Cautiously, Jack looked around, running his snake-hook through the sparse branches along the path.

The woods at this point came up to the back fence of one of the last houses, residing on the outer-perimeter of the neighborhood. It was a wooden fence, and Jack walked along, unhappily noting the wide gaps between and under the boards – accessible for a slender snake.

Grabbing a post, Jack pulled himself up to look over into the residence's backyard. He could see through the windows into the kitchen, and partly into the living room, but there was no obvious activity.

Jack hopped back down, circling to the edge of the fence where a stone path had been built leading to the front of the house.

The family and all the neighbors would have to be warned. At least one of the mambas had been in the immediate area within the last few hours. He would have to go door-to-door. Based on public response so-far, he wasn't looking forward to that.

He paused a moment, wondering if he should just let the police do it.

No, he decided – there was urgency here. Jack would call the police, and let them do rounds, but right now, the people in *this* house, at least, as well as the immediate neighbors, needed to be alerted right away.

But as he walked around to the front porch, Jack saw the door to the main entrance was standing ajar.

Just inside, he saw a man lying on the floor.

CHAPTER 3

Everybody in the house was dead.

Jack pushed the front door open, and he could see five bodies strewn across the floor – two adults and three kids.

As he stepped cautiously inside, the scene told its own story.

It was the sort of thing that happened in rural Africa, where humans encroached on mamba territory. The snake would come into native huts at night, looking for rodents, slithering from room to room, striking quickly at the slightest disturbance, often not even noticed by the sleeping victim. There were even cases where mambas seemed to deliberately target every last individual in the house, even babies in cribs, possibly out of a sense of territoriality.

But be it malevolence or defensiveness, either way, in the morning, the entire household would be found dead.

As Jack carefully scanned the room, he saw the rear sliding door was open. It was a sunny day and there were also windows open in the kitchen. They had been cooking dinner. The pot on the kettle was still boiling.

Keeping his eyes carefully on every corner, Jack stepped into the kitchen and shut the stove off.

The pot wasn't even boiled over, yet. This hadn't happened very long ago. Probably no more than ten or fifteen minutes. If he'd walked-up a few minutes earlier, he might have been able to save them. He had antivenin on hand, and it was usually quite effective.

On the 'good' side of mamba-envenomation – a somewhat dubious statement – if you *did* get treatment, after-effects were minimal, compared to the massive, acid-burn tissue-damage you'd get from your average viper-bite – neurotoxin versus hemotoxin. Mamba-bites sometimes showed varying effects, just because of popping chemistry, but they were atypical.

Jack guessed the snake had come in through the back, following its nose. Based on the orientation of the bodies, the kids had been watching television, and the mamba had most likely simply crawled past. Jack could picture the screams, the mother coming running from the kitchen, the father from somewhere in the back, perhaps the garage.

The mamba would have struck repeatedly, lashing out aggressively at its antagonists.

And as Jack looked closer, both mom and dad showed blood from small bite marks in multiple spots on their face, neck, and hands. That implied someone reaching for the snake, probably upon finding the thing in the process of killing their kids.

Face and neck bites would maximize the speed and effect of the venom. The mother was sprawled nearly on top of the children. The father had made it far enough to partially open the front door, before he collapsed.

The kids were all young. Jack guessed the two sisters no more than six and seven. The older brother was maybe nine. With a combined body-weight under a hundred-pounds, they wouldn't have lasted long, and probably would have been dead in minutes.

As he analyzed the likely scenario, he decided ten minutes wouldn't have made much difference after all. Not for the kids. Certainly not for the parents with multiple face and neck bites.

The actual encounter probably would have lasted less than a minute or two.

Which, of course, meant the mamba was still somewhere nearby.

The female was theoretically a bit chubby with eggs, so hopefully that would make her a little easier to handle, because it would certainly make her more irritable.

She would be a bit smaller too. Mambas were the opposite of pythons, where the big constrictors were the females – a product of a species where males didn't compete for mating rights, engaging instead in group mating-balls. Male mambas, like all elapids, fought for their mates, and were thus, typically larger.

A smaller female, however, was not necessarily better. It cut down on a snake's striking range, but also made it easier to hide, and more difficult to grab.

Jack spent about twenty-minutes hunting her up.

The mamba had retreated to the master-bedroom, and was resting comfortably between the sheets. Jack spotted the snake's gray-slate body almost right away, a loop of its coil peeking out from between the white linens like a bicycle tire.

Jack approached cautiously. He held his catch bag on the end of a three-foot rod, positioned in front of him like a shield. His snake-hook was in his other hand, fitted with a squeeze-grip clamp. Basic procedure was to grip the snake behind the head, making sure to get close enough so that the fangs couldn't reach back over the length of the shaft. Then you pinned it down, and with the catch-bag fitted over your hand like a glove, you gripped the snake directly behind its jaws, and pulled the bag on backwards over its head, in the manner of pulling on a pillowcase.

You didn't let go until the opening to the bag was twisted and knotted, and when you released, you had to pull your hand away quickly. Mambas, among venomous snakes, were particularly known for biting handlers through bags.

Physically, it was a very easy process. You just had to make sure you did it right, because if you did it wrong, you were dead.

Using the tongs, Jack gently pulled the bed-sheet up and back.

It was not gently enough. The mamba started from its cover.

Jack realized he stood between the snake and the bedroom door. The female was just under eight-feet long, and most of her length was still under the blankets.

Moving with the sort of unthinking reflex you always *hoped* would be there, Jack pressed his hook quickly down on the sheets, pinning the mamba down.

But nearly four feet of neck was free – that was enough to reach him.

Jack saw the wide-open, jet-black mouth that gave the species its name, as the deceptively tiny head snapped at him like a whip. He parried with the catch-bag, bringing it quickly in front of his vulnerable hand, turning the opening sideways into what looked like a nice safe place to escape.

In the blink of an eye, the mamba took the bait. It lurched towards the bag. Jack guided it along with the hook, and the snake's entire, pool-cue-thin length slid out from under the covers, into the bag like an unwinding kite-line. Once the mamba's body was entirely inside, he pulled his hand quickly back and away. Then he twisted the catch-bag over its own opening, three times, trapping the snake inside.

Consciously holding the bag arms-length away, Jack could already see the tiny pin-pricks of fangs poking through the fabric, barely a quarter-inch long. Venom squirted, staining the bag's white cloth.

Jack felt the post-catch rush of adrenaline. He took a second to relax, allowing himself a moment's relief, simply that he'd caught the snake.

Unfortunately, as she'd slid her length out from under the sheets, Jack had seen that she was no longer gravid.

Sometime in the two weeks since she'd escaped the venom-farm, the female mamba had laid her eggs.

The Institute was three-miles away. The nest could be anywhere. Mambas didn't guard their young. The mother just laid and then simply abandoned the nest, taking off and never seeing them again.

A surviving egg-clutch could be a dozen or more, and hatchlings could soon be slithering anywhere from the open fields, to the woods, or into the neighborhoods, as tiny and unassuming as garter snakes, each one a potential death-sentence inside half-an-hour.

Jack shut his eyes, picturing kids chasing them with a glass jar, just like he'd done after garters as a boy.

At least he had the mother snake secured.

He turned back to the living room and the grim scene that waited there.

Now he had to deal with all the dead people.

He pulled out his phone and called the police. He told them to send an ambulance, but there was no need to run a siren.

Then he tapped out a group-message, copying in Janice, as well as Chuck and Lindsey.

"*We've got a nest,*" it said.

CHAPTER 4

The break-in at the Institute was two weeks ago, almost directly on the heels of James Warden's release from jail.

Jack had been less than pleased to see him let go, after serving only sixty-days of an allotted six-months. Jack supposed the Institute was lucky the man had done any time at all, although the steady harassment from his acolytes during his confinement was hardly a respite. Jack was on his third set of tires, along with a new windshield.

But the break-in took it up a notch. Several notches, actually.

It was so frustratingly unnecessary. The Institute was already shutting down. Was it just about biting their ankles on the way out?

Just in sheer property damage alone, vandalism had already cost the Institute, and by extension, the university and the taxpayers, tens of thousands. Of course, the press didn't *call* them 'vandals' – they were 'protesting' – 'students exercising their First-Amendment rights'.

Except, of course, for the ones that weren't. There were also the anarchist assholes who only lived in town because they were tolerated.

With only a few weeks before the Institute was scheduled to close, Jack had been clinging to the naive hope they could get through it without any major incident. Part of him knew better. The thuggish element had infiltrated and was on display early-on. It was more or less what put James Warden up the river for his sixty-days.

That particular incident actually started with Lindsey, although Chuck again managed to get punched – more than once, in fact.

The initial flash-point, didn't even have anything to do with the university, or the Institute. It started with Lindsey's own quarterback boyfriend – and, of course, Chuck, who had an obvious crush on Lindsey, just as Jack imagined every young man that knew her also did.

That was another area where Jack could relate. His own Freshman-year-beating at the hands of the starting lineup mirrored the incident that blew up at the little cafe just the other side of the highway. It was a local-brand coffeehouse frequented by commuters, right near where they'd built the new transit-station.

Lindsey's own football-hero was an almost insolently handsome young man named Bradley Brown. He was currently gearing-up for his senior year at the state university, and since the med-school was affiliated, he was considered secondhand alumni. He was also Dean Herman Brown's son, so he was popular locally.

But it was likewise that specific relation which sent the cafe-incident into extra-innings. Left alone, the altercation probably would have been minor. Unfortunately, James Warden and several of his friends had been in the house that day too.

What happened was simple enough. The place was walking distance of the Institute, so Lindsey and Chuck had gone there for lunch.

Chuck was being a little jerky-cute, as he tended to be around Lindsey, and made a rather mild derogatory comment about "your dumb-ass, caveman boyfriend," unaware that Brad had just walked in with several teammates, right in time to hear it.

Seeing Lindsey's pained expression, Chuck had turned to see Brad standing behind him, a moment before he was snatched out of the booth and pushed up against the wall.

Jack had met Brad Brown on a number of occasions, and never thought of him as a particularly hard guy. But the blatant disrespect in front of his teammates, not to mention the presumed familiarity with his girl, prompted a dutiful response. Lindsey told Jack later Brad had already remarked that he was "getting tired of that little weasel sucking around."

Which Jack had to admit wasn't *entirely* inaccurate.

He also had to admit to some insider information that might explain some of Brad's insecurity.

Lindsey had confided in Jack that she and Bradley Brown were 'not-quite engaged' because she didn't quite *want* to be.

Lindsey told Jack months ago, long before the incident in the cafe, that she'd actually been cooling on Bradley for a long time.

On paper, he was perfect. He was handsome, intelligent, and he was heading for the big time – the NFL was waiting for him. That was not to mention, he already had the attention of legions of groupies.

Lindsey had never caught him in any indiscretions, although she knew the secrecy for road-trips with those teams were tribal.

But fidelity wasn't really the issue. The fact was Brad Brown was very much an alpha male. That meant his woman was *his* woman. That was why he snatched Chuck out of the booth that day, even if Lindsey didn't think he really intended to hurt him.

More than that, it also seemed he'd picked *her* for the same reason. Lindsey was the bombshell on campus the year he became a star, and so he chose her as his rightful prize.

She would be lying, Lindsey had admitted to Jack, if that didn't appeal to the cavewoman in her. But it was too much dominance.

And in the end, it was superficial – all about image. As one of her friends had told her, "He'll love you forever, or until you put on twenty-pounds."

The fact that Bradley Brown was headed for fame and fortune, also meant a lot of public attention. And after the small taste she'd gotten, just from the city press, from being a local football-hero's girlfriend, Lindsey really didn't want all that came with being an NFL bride.

In a way, she told Jack, it would be a kindness to simply let him go and live the superstar life that was only there to be had by a select few.

She had, as she mentioned to Jack, just the other day, so far, been just a little too chickenshit to cut the cord.

Jack suspected Chuck had caught wind of this sentiment, and gotten his hopes up.

The crush was painfully obvious in the younger man's eyes, and when Chuck once asked – hypothetically – if he thought a girl like Lindsey might ever be into him, Jack had answered honestly.

"*No*," he said emphatically. "I don't. At *all*."

Then he told his beat-up-by-the-football-team story, in the offhand hope he could curtail any drama going forward.

No such luck. The scene at the cafe was already set-up like a house of cards.

To be fair, Brad hadn't hit Chuck yet when James Warden and his friends got involved. Then things escalated quickly.

Different versions of the story muddied the water in terms of actual provocation. Brad and Chuck by themselves probably wouldn't have gone much further. Lindsey was already on her feet, moving to separate them and, as Brad said later, "I was just shaking some respect out of the little twerp."

But James Warden knew who Brad was. Seizing the opportunity to posture, he stepped forward dramatically, demanding Brad, "Leave that kid alone."

Brad had responded curtly with, "Mind your own business, asshole."

Both factions came together at once. Brad's teammates filed-in behind him, as James Warden's friends came up out of their corner booth, making four on each side. The little cafe erupted into a saloon-style brawl.

The police were called, windows were broken, and arrests were made. But in the end, the security cameras showed James Warden throwing first.

Chuck got punched randomly four times, once by a footballer, and three times by one of the activists who hollered out, "Piece of *shit!*" as they pounded away.

But it was that first punch by James Warden that made the difference with local D.A.. And that was even after being given every benefit of the doubt. He and his friends spent the rest of that day in jail, but were released the next morning. James Warden had responded by promptly arranging one of his flash-protests outside Dean Brown's office at the med-school on the hill, actually hanging both him and Bradley Brown in effigy.

Dean Brown, who had by now filed an official restraining order, took the somewhat heretical opinion, only embraced by academics who have it happen on their own front lawn, that such demonstrations were deliberately threatening and therefore not free-speech. He called the police, and this time, when James Warden was taken into custody, he didn't walk right back out again. On top of the charges being filed by the cafe-owner, the D.A. decided it was time James Warden got a time-out.

All of which had the effect of making what started out as a cause into a personal-issue on both sides.

But the break-in escalated things to a whole new level.

The dead people should have been enough, but the fact that one of them was Liz Williams was a wild-card. Where the ultimate weight of her father's influence would ultimately fall wasn't yet clear, but Jack was certain the city was looking into it more furtively than they had his slashed tires, or Chuck's skateboard-cracked head.

So far, James Warden was laying low. Reports said he was 'wanted for questioning', although they still hadn't mentioned a warrant for his arrest.

But now there was a dead family of five.

All hell was going to break loose. Jack's phone call had already lit the fuse.

In the distance, he heard approaching sirens. He'd told them not to bother, but they were lit-up for urgency anyway.

With the mamba in the catch-bag, Jack headed outside to meet them.

Already, neighbors down the street were poking their heads out.

CHAPTER 5

Jack came out of the house with the mamba in the catch-bag, waiting on the porch as the emergency vehicles pulled up, two police cruisers and an ambulance. They shut off their sirens but left on the blinking lights. Jack raised the catch-bag and waved.

The police and paramedics all knew him by now. He was mortally certain the press was right on their heels.

He'd hoped to spend the afternoon hunting for the mamba-nest, and had been debating calling Chuck or Lindsey, perhaps both of them, to help scour the immediate area, but now he suspected he would be stuck in officialdom for the remainder of the day.

Down the street, the neighbors were starting to come out of their houses.

Among them, he saw none other than Addy's mom, Mrs. Janelle Robins.

Just perfect. Jack groaned aloud.

For the moment, she was hanging back with the others, regarding the emergency vehicles with the same fearful doubt, but she was eyeing Jack venomously.

Jack spared a moment, eying her back, before he turned to meet the police and ambulance-team.

He recognized the first two officers as the transit-cops who arrested him after he'd punched-out young Addy Robins, a pair of by-the-book clones named Cates and Hammond. Ignoring Jack, the two of them moved to cordon-off the front yard from the curious neighbors.

The second pair of officers, Jack knew from the night of the break-in at the Institute. The driver was Officer Benton, about Jack's age. His partner was a female officer about five years younger, Officer Jensen, a hard-body, who rocked her spandex, teaching kick-boxing at the local gym. They both eyed Jack as he approached, holding the catch-bag at arms-length.

"Is that what I think it is?" Officer Benton asked.

Jack nodded, and briefly described the scene in the house.

Benton groaned. Officer Jensen turned and nodded to the two medics, who started unloading their stretchers.

"You got it cleared out, right?" Benton said as the medics made their way into the house.

"Yeah," Jack said, holding up the bag. They could see the coils of the snake rustling inside. "But there's more bad news. This snake was a female. And sometime in the last two weeks, somewhere in the three-miles back to the Institute, she's already laid probably about a dozen eggs."

Officer Benton let out a slow breath.

"How long before they hatch?"

Jack shrugged.

"About sixty to ninety days. We've got time. But we definitely don't want them hatching."

"Are the hatchlings dangerous?" Officer Jensen asked.

Jack nodded gravely.

"Every bit as venomous as an adult," he said. "In fact, the young ones are sometimes worse, because they don't hold back. They inject their full venom load."

Jack glanced down at his catch-bag. For the moment, the snake inside lay quiet.

Officers Hammond and Cates were cordoning off the yard, even as the crowd of wide-eyed neighbors encroached.

There was a horrified murmur as the front door to the house opened and the first of the bodies was brought out, sheet pulled over the head – the father.

"Oh my God," a woman's voice said, "that's *Bob*."

Jack realized he didn't even know the family's name. He'd given the police dispatcher the address on the door. Now he saw the name on the mailbox was 'Connors'.

Bob Connors. Now he knew him.

"They're all dead, aren't they?" a shrill, familiar voice chirped from the crowd.

Jack turned to find Mrs. Robins standing up front, near the police-line, eying him accusingly.

"What have you *done?*" she hissed.

Jack sighed deeply. The family in this house – the Connors – was dead because the Institute's security was criminally circumvented by activists – just like her son, a young man who had committed felonious assault right in front of Jack's own eyes. Yet, Mrs. Robins glared with unabashed judgment.

A defensive reaction? Jack wondered. Just a mother/kid thing?

From the house behind him, a second stretcher was brought out, a smaller lump under the sheet – Mrs. Connors this time. There was another murmur from the crowd. Jack heard the name, '*Ellen*', echo in hushed tones .

Standing up front, Mrs. Robins eyed Jack unwaveringly.

"This is *your* fault," she said. "You're as good as a *murderer.*"

For a moment, Jack felt the impulse to just step over the police-tape, hand her his snake-hook and the mamba bag, and say, "Here. *You* do it."

He guessed that all by itself would probably be enough to get her killed. He could see the mamba biting right through the bag. She would probably scream, drop the bag, and get bit several more times before allowing the mamba to escape.

Jack sighed. He'd probably earned himself an hour in Purgatory just for the thought. But he at least allowed himself one nasty look back at her before he turned to see the press-wagon come rolling around the corner, urgent as an ambulance. Now he cringed.

As the news-van pulled up beside the two police cars, Jack's eyes narrowed, recognizing the fretful, earnest-looking field-anchor in the front seat, Leslie Daniels – a young woman Jack did not particularly like.

A cookie-cutter, two-years out of college, working her first on-camera job for the local station, she was known to speak weightily and profoundly on both local politics and global policy.

And based on how many times she'd run Jack's own mug-shut, he'd be happy enough to toss the mamba-bag in her direction too.

Okay. *Two* hours in Purgatory.

Leslie Daniels was climbing out of the van, turning her eyes quickly to Jack and Officer Benton. She moved to step across the police-line, but Officer Jensen intercepted her.

"Not just yet, ma'am."

Jack turned to Officer Benton as they both said together, "*You* talk to them."

Benton waved his hand.

"*You're* the expert," he said.

"*You're* the authority," Jack returned.

Behind them, with unfortunate timing for the cameras, the front door to the Connors' house opened again, this time bringing out the first of the three kids.

The gathered crowd fluttered together.

Mrs. Robins' voice rose above the rest, now directed to Officers Benton and Jensen, as she pointed at Jack, who continued to walk around free.

"Aren't you going to arrest him?" she shouted, her voice suddenly teary. "How many dead children do you need?"

Jack glared at her through slitted eyes, glancing down at the bag in his hand.

Okay. *Three* hours in Purgatory.

The catch-bag jerked, as if the mamba was responding to his thoughts.

Taking a breath, Jack turned, resigned, to Leslie Daniels and her cameras.

CHAPTER 6

Jack arrived back at the Institute later that day.

The building was sparsely populated. With the place closing down, the Venom Lab was the only section of the building that was actually operating on a daily basis anymore. The animal-research labs were already on minimal staff, simply just tending to the upkeep for the remaining live animals.

Most of the loose monkeys were recovered after a few days. They actually just showed-up at feeding time. The cats and dogs were still running stray. There was a brief scare that these animals might be infected with some exotic manufactured disease – more *gain-function* – but Dean Brown held several comforting news-briefs, talking specifically to Leslie Daniels, whose fretful, concerned face turned reassuringly to the camera, telling her audience that there was no danger.

Jack didn't know about that, but there *were* still a couple-dozen-plus extremely deadly exotic serpents roaming the surrounding neighborhoods. Not to mention a number of venomous scorpions, spiders, and hornets.

So maybe a *little* danger.

And the hell of it was, another six weeks and the Venom Farm was closing down. If the break-in had happened two months from now, the snakes would have all been gone. But now it meant that they had a limited window to round-up all the getaways.

The facility would have actually already been closed, except for an effort to coordinate with an upcoming Reptile-Expo.

It was a yearly event that focused on venomous exotics, and the location of the Venom Lab in Silver Lake was originally chosen, in part, because of its proximity to the popular annual event, and theoretically a positive community reception.

Initially, that actually *had* been the case. The Venom Lab operated a high-profile booth out of the Expo every year. The lab was intended to complement Venom-One out of Florida, the nation's primary antivenin source for a variety of exotic snakes.

Antivenin was usually stocked by medical facilities based on local species. But the problem with exotics, was that you might find them anywhere. And the drawback in the Venom-One operation was that, if you got bit by a pet Asian cobra in Washington state, with the appropriate antivenin a cross-continental flight away in Florida, you might easily be dead before it got there.

If the Venom Lab worked out well, they also intended to open another location somewhere in the mid-western states.

Local troubles, however, had bumped up moving plans. In the short-term, the snakes were going to mostly be transported to Idaho, into a privately-funded building near the industrial areas, close to the Boise Airport. The site was supposedly temporary, but Jack was hoping they could just simply reopen there and stay.

He'd flown over once, several weeks ago, and the facility was ready to operate. In fact, Jack would be its only personnel until he could bring someone in locally. Neither Chuck or Lindsey intended to move.

That was also why they hadn't started shipping any of their snakes out there yet. Jack had been waiting in town for the Expo to be over.

One of the other services the Venom Lab conveniently provided at the yearly event was snake-adoption, and he always wanted to be on-site for that.

The idea was to provide free, responsible adoption of animals that might otherwise be killed, or released into the wild, with no questions asked about legality.

Invasive species, in many cases from released pets, were a huge problem in places like Florida, a near-perfect habitat for exotic herps. Oregon's Willamette Valley was not a dream-home like the Everglades, but it was certainly livable. Even in the relatively frigid hilltops, there were indigenous rattlesnakes. And if they could make a go, there's no reason a cobra couldn't.

The Expo gave the Venom Lab a platform and an avenue for their adoption program that had worked out well for years. But it was an operation Jack preferred to oversee himself. People were known to come in with anything from bushmasters, to spitting cobras, to reticulated pythons, and some of these were not particularly well contained, coiled-up in gunny-sacks, or plastic garbage cans and cardboard shipping boxes.

There was an infamous case in Florida, a black-market deal, where a guy was selling a black mamba, which he carried in a simple pillowcase. A midnight transaction on the side of the road, the buyer was bit, and was damn lucky to be alive so he could face charges.

Stories like that literally gave Jack the shivers.

He reflexively glanced over his shoulder, where the mamba was secured in its catch-bag. Even locked in his trunk, it always made him a little nervous to have the snake at his back.

Lindsey's Mustang was parked in its spot, alone in the vacant lot, as Jack pulled in. She and Chuck had been out snake-hunting when they got Jack's first text, and they'd each returned with a pair of Asian cobras, all four escapees now secured back in their cages.

Janice had also sent a group text, calling for an online staff-meeting as soon as Jack made it back.

When Jack walked in, Chuck and Lindsey were sitting in their little break-room outside the main lab, watching him on TV. He was talking to Leslie Daniels, still holding his mamba-bag at arm's length. This was the moment when he'd held the bag up just a little too close, after she'd thrust the microphone into his face.

"Careful," his on-screen self cautioned, "this is one of the deadliest animals on Earth I'm holding here."

He brought the bag up for the camera, showing the mamba's fangs poking through the cloth, staining the fabric in venom.

"The amount she's injecting," Jack said, "would kill you inside half-an-hour."

Leslie Daniels paled, and stepped back a more respectful distance.

Lindsey turned and eyed Jack, reproachfully bemused.

"I saw you swing that bag a little close to her," she said. "You told me you'd fire any one of us for something like that."

"I would," Jack agreed.

Then Lindsey's eyes fell to the catch-bag still in Jack's hands, and she shuddered. She was just a bit phobic about the mambas.

There was writhing movement in the bag as the jostling agitated the nervous snake, and once again, fangs poked through the thin fabric.

"Could you please put her away?" Lindsey said.

"Sorry."

Jack carried the snake over to its cage. This was just as tricky as getting it into the bag, if you didn't know what you were doing. The tank was a terrarium with a top lid, looking like a large fish-tank. A mamba didn't actually require much space.

Deftly, Jack dropped the top of the catch-bag into the open tank before untwisting it from the bottom, making sure to use the hook, and sliding the snake into its cage.

Both Chuck and Lindsey watched, riveted, during that half-second of transfer. They knew Jack was always meticulous about his grip, the placement of his hands and bag, but it only took a moment for things to go dramatically wrong.

Chuck actually liked working with the mambas, although Jack only let him do it under his personal supervision. The kid even professed a desire to own one someday, although Jack knew he was probably not likely to be granted a permit for private ownership. He had one of the more unfortunate '*got-bit*' stories.

To be fair, it was not a shameful badge. Almost everybody who worked with venomous snakes had a '*got-bit*' story. Lindsey was a very notable exception, and her clean record was as much to do with her youth as her skill. In this field, time and odds were never on your side. In point of fact, Chuck's own story was poignantly similar to Jack's own, at least the first incident, which, like Jack's, was only at secondhand.

But both of them had lost a brother.

Jack understood psychology well enough, and he remembered something one of his martial-arts instructors told him: “No one does this unless something scares them first.”

Interest in deadly serpents was a fascination rooted in fear, even to the point of obsession. Perhaps it was ultimately a need to beat it. Why else would you fixate on something that could so easily kill you?

In Chuck's case, he'd been hiking in the hills with his older brother – a Scouts-thing. His brother stumbled into a rattlesnake nest and was bitten several times. Chuck, barely ten-years-old, had wandered back home on his own, where he had simply walked, wide-eyed and blank-faced into his kitchen. He had been uncommunicative, but his mother had called the police, and a search found his brother a short-while later, still lying in the midst of the rattler nest.

Chuck's 'great interest' had begun that day. He was raised in the hills of northern California, the son of a single-mother who worked, and who was also surprisingly supportive of her son's obsessive new passion, even after he started a venomous herp collection of his own.

At first it was rattlesnakes, starting with a baby Mojave that he caught after watching an episode of *Crocodile Hunter* on Nickelodeon. By the time he was sixteen, his room had half-a-dozen rattlers, as well as a copperhead, a cottonmouth, and a coral snake – all American species.

After spending the last six-years chasing rattlers in the hills, he had become fairly adept at handling them. But now he would venture into, not just 'hot' herps, but exotics. And right out of the gate, was a three-foot Gaboon adder, purchased nowhere but that year's reptile-expo.

The Gaboon was going to be the jewel of his collection, and owning one was a literal lifetime dream. It was one of the most notorious of vipers, with the longest fangs, the highest-venom yield, and a terrible tissue-destroying toxin, that also produced cobra-like neurotoxic effects, all delivered with a strike faster than the blink of an eye.

Fortunately, the snake was extremely sluggish, and often had to be stepped-on to provoke a strike. Its habitat was also very remote jungle, allowing it very little contact with humans, so it accounted for few bites or fatalities in its native Africa.

Unfortunately, in Chuck's bedroom, his own particular adder was apparently still agitated from the entire process of delivery. It was the second day, after Chuck brought it home, that he took the first bite.

He described it the same way every handler does, who had never been bit before.

"I couldn't believe it," he told Jack. "I felt the stab of the fangs and it was like getting hit with a hard punch."

Gaboons were extremely thick, squat vipers, and could spring into a very powerful strike.

"And, oh my *God*," Chuck said, showing Jack the scars on his arms, "the *pain*. It was like fire."

Extremely fortunately, Chuck had the foresight to notify the local hospital of the potential need of antivenin for this specific exotic species. It had, in fact, been the Venom Lab that had sent the Gaboon-serum down. Treatment had required four entire-vials.

Chuck had suffered a great deal of swelling, but the sort of tissue-damage normally associated with a Gaboon-bite was averted by the prompt attention, and he had gone home the next day.

Less than two weeks later, he took his second bite, on the other hand this time. Just a nick, but his whole hand swelled up like a balloon. They'd used up half their store of Gaboon adder serum just treating his last bite alone. This time the Venom Lab air-lifted extra-serum, as they went through the remaining vials in an hour.

Again, Chuck luckily avoided massive scarring, being on the receiving end of immediate treatment.

The third bite, nearly three weeks later, cost him his snake, and was the most serious of the three, this time catching Chuck in the lower leg.

Jack had seen the scarring the other two bites had left on Chuck's hand – ugly, gnarled holes right at the fang-mark, with all the surrounding tissue taking on the cast of once having been burned. But it was all superficial, his arm and fingers worked perfectly.

The bite on the leg left him the tiniest bit club-footed. He had been holding the snake by the tail, preparing to clean out its cage, when the three-foot body turned on a dime, finding him once again, this time burying one fang deep into his calf.

A significant amount of venom was injected – damage to the tendons and muscles was permanent. Ten vials of antivenin this time, along with a four-day hospital stay. And during this convalescence, the state – in fact, in the person of Jack, himself – had gone to Chuck's residence and confiscated his snake.

They still had that same Gaboon at the Institute today. Jack, who kept in contact with Chuck during his convalescence, actually had the young man out on occasion to visit his former pet, and they kept up their correspondence after Chuck began pursuing his own herp-major in college.

Chuck's unfortunate incident with the Gaboon viper had almost blocked his internship. Dean Herman Brown, himself, directly objected to his appointment, and if Jack hadn't interceded on his behalf, he would have been turned down.

To this day, Jack pointedly did not have Chuck handle his old Gaboon. The species was not generally considered the most difficult to work with, because it was lethargic to the point of stuporous, but its strike was near-instantaneous, so controlling it was a simple matter of gauging its striking range, and staying outside.

Chuck's difficulties with the Gaboon were rather like how some fighters can have problems with certain styles. Some handlers had more difficulty with some species than others. Jack knew an experienced snake-keeper out of Thailand, who took repeated bites from a Russell's viper, to the point where he had to be likewise segregated from the species in the reptile park where he worked.

At the Venom Lab, Jack sort of acted as the safety-net for the other two, having confident experience with all the species on-site.

Like Lindsey, Jack had never actually taken a bite. Like Chuck's first incident with the rattlers, Jack's own got-bit story was also at secondhand, and every bit as grim.

It was another rattlesnake-story. Jack had been eleven, camping in the hills with his own older brother and one of his friends.

During the night, Jack woke to find a rattlesnake crawling on top of him, and another poking its head out of his sleeping bag.

He would never forget the sheer ice-cold paralysis that had gripped him when he heard that ominous rattle in the dark, right up next to his ear. He couldn't speak, he could barely breathe. Afraid even to call out to his brother, he lay there in the dark for hours.

His father found them the next morning. Jack had still been lying terrified and shaking in his sleeping bag, the rattlers now long gone. His brother and his friend were both dead, bitten sometime during the night.

And just like Chuck, Jack's interest in venomous snakes had bloomed after that.

Oddly, rattlers didn't bother him so much these days. Their striking range was the first thing he'd mastered. Just like martial arts, evading an opponent was simply about observing his limb-length and proportions, and judging where the strike had to come from. If you stood outside that arc, it didn't matter how fast the strike came.

You had to judge accurately, of course. A lot of these hot-herps hit quite a bit harder than any fistful of knuckles. Or starting lineup of footballers, for that matter. And you had to see them coming.

But just like Lindsey, despite his traumatic incident, he'd never actually been bitten, himself. So that made the two of them a pair of unicorns, working under the same roof. His colleagues – Janice was one – would always remind him of the old saying in the field that, the longer you went without getting bit, made it more likely the one that gets you was going to kill you.

Neither Jack or Lindsey particularly liked that joke, although Jack always laughed dutifully, making sure not to challenge the jinx. '*Eventually*' was a scary word.

What you had to do was trust in procedure. Jack always made sure there was never a situation with a hot-herp that came down to luck.

First and foremost, he never, *ever*, broke the range rule.

Snakes as a whole were actually pretty easy to handle if you just stuck to that simple principle. Jack compared it to shark-attack – no one had ever been bit by a shark while lying on the beach. You had to be in the water.

There were, however, critters that broke the rules.

In Australia, you might be safe from sharks on the beach, but a saltwater crocodile might walk right up on the sand and pull you in.

And for Jack, the worst rule breaker was always the mamba.

You didn't have to break the range-rule – the mamba broke it for you, with that deceptive length, hidden by that pool-cue-thin body, springing forward like an arrow on a string, tapping you with fangs that might be less than a quarter inch on a thumb-sized head.

That was to say nothing of writhing little hatchlings the size of garter snakes, lashing out with tiny fangs that would just barely cut, like stepping on splinters of broken glass – and the hatchlings always bit with their full load. You might not even feel the bite walking across a field, but be dead before you got to the other side.

On TV, Leslie Daniels was interviewing the Connors family's neighbors. Jack recognized one of the young mothers who'd been hovering behind the police line that afternoon. A subtitle identified her as "Susan Burnett, neighbor'.

"My kids," Mrs. Burnett was telling Leslie, "said they saw a big black snake in the yard." She half-laughed. "I told them just to leave it alone."

Her shudder was visible on TV.

You could hear Mrs. Robins in the background, her voice raised, mostly repetitive, about how *somebody* needed to be arrested.

"You know," Jack said unhappily, joining Lindsey and Chuck in front of the TV, "she's talking about all of *us*."

Chuck shrugged.

"Well," he said, "they had her on earlier. So far, she's just mentioned *you*."

And even as he said it, the screen switched to past footage of Jack himself, a montage of scenes from previous years at the Expo, handling cobras and vipers. And as if that hadn't given everyone a good enough look at his face, the screen now switched to the mugshot taken on the day of his arrest.

"Doctor Jonathon 'Jack' Wright of the Institute was also previously arrested for the assault of a minor, during a clash with activist groups, several weeks ago," Leslie Daniels' narrative supplied, but not offering any circumstances.

Jack cursed under his breath.

At that moment, his phone beeped in his pocket, followed a moment later by Chuck and Lindsey's. It was Janice' incoming conference call.

They all sat their phones on the table and sat down as Janice appeared on their screens.

"Okay," Janice said, "first off. Everybody okay, today? Jack?"

"Well," Jack replied, "I've had better days. I walked in on five dead people this morning, including three kids. There's at least one crazy woman in the neighborhood who wants to hang someone for it. And based on the news coverage so far, I'm hoping I won't be walking out into an angry mob when I try and go home tonight."

"Yeah," Janice said, "about that. I just got word directly from Dean Brown. The Institute is closing down at the end of the week."

There was a moment of silence in the room. Today was Thursday. You might call that short-notice. They all knew this was coming, but this felt very much like being cut-loose.

"Dean Brown," Janice said, "is concerned that there may be violence, and doesn't want anybody on-site if this thing blows up."

"What about the Expo?" Jack asked. "That's Saturday."

"We will not be having a booth there this year," Janice said. "We will maintain a presence, for people who come to drop off or donate their exotics, but after this weekend, everything we've got ships out to Idaho."

Jack glanced at the others. That meant *him* as well.

"What about all the getaways?" he asked.

Janice tossed her hands onscreen.

"I don't know what to tell you," she said. "You've got a couple of days. Do what you can. After that, I guess it's the city-parks department's problem."

"You're not serious."

"My understanding is that they're going to have a town-council meeting next week about hiring an outside specialist. The university is pulling completely out. They don't want any of us anywhere near."

Jack shut his eyes, resisting anger.

He thought about the deadly creatures still prowling the surrounding landscape, and the reason they were there was because of the same idiots who were forcing them to shut down.

And when the next bodies turned up – and Jack now believed there would be no stopping it – there would be not one moment of self-reproach.

There *would* no doubt be anger and blame, of course. And with the damned press practically inciting it.

Jack supposed he was lucky. After this weekend, he would be gone.

It was possible, he supposed, that some of the activists might follow the cause into Idaho, although the local authorities there were not as accommodating to radical acting-out.

But he also couldn't discount the possibility of criminal prosecution, if the local D.A. heard enough preaching from the likes of Mrs. Robins, and maybe a few of her friends, to sway her in that direction. Or worse, someone like George Williams.

A public prosecution would bring glowing press coverage. What was more worrisome was the possibility of the public cheering it on.

"Jack," Janice said on-screen, "for what it's worth, I'm sorry about all of this. None of it is your fault."

"Thanks, Janice," Jack said, and they ended the conference call.

Jack turned to the others.

"Well," he said, "you heard it. We've got until the end of the week." He shrugged. "Until then, nothing's changed. Stay alive first. Don't let short-time syndrome get you killed."

Chuck and Lindsey both nodded somberly.

Jack ran down a mental tally of the getaways still missing – several cobras, including the king, the taipan, the second mamba, not to mention that mamba nest was now out there somewhere.

On TV, the news had switched back to a neighborhood view of the Connors family house, including the crowd gathered outside the police-line, with Mrs. Robins holding her fist up.

"Neighbors are angry," Leslie Daniels' voice-over intoned. "And they are demanding action."

Behind her, the crowd was starting to cheer Mrs. Robins on. Jack saw Mrs. Burnett clapping her hands.

Jack only hoped he found enough escaped seven-step snakes to save a few of those angry peasants' lives before they grabbed their pitchforks and ran him out of town.

But he was beginning to have his doubts.

CHAPTER 7

It stormed hard the day of the break-in.

In the aftermath, it was even given a Biblical spin on the local news – Leslie Daniels again, playing-up a 'cleansing of Babylon' angle sort of cross-bred with the 'snakes in the garden'.

Jack didn't know about any cleansing of Babylon, but he would grant at least three Darwin Awards, all awarded at the scene, and all caught on film.

If anything, the storm might have actually saved their lives if it had only continued into the evening hours. The intruders had entered the outer security doors using stolen pass-codes, which wouldn't have operated during the storm because the power had gone out.

The system had been in reboot, so the security cameras didn't turn back on right away, so some of the incident was uncertain, but the vandals could be clearly seen entering the Venom Lab.

Cameras down the hallways revealed the loosed dogs, cats, and monkeys, and all the exit doors propped open. This would have been about ten minutes after the access-codes had been activated.

The three masked vandals had actually been mugging at the security cameras when they finally came on, obviously believing they'd been on-video all along, no doubt expecting the footage of their venture to be recorded, and made public. It was all about the show, after all, being *seen* letting these animals out.

Of course, the show got a little better than they probably expected once they got to the Venom Lab.

You could hear them on video, as they wandered the rows of cages, peering in at the menagerie of spiders, and scorpions, and snakes.

"Oh, shit, what's in here? Look at this!"

Then the fire started, and the marveling turned to shrieks and the cursing went shrill. You could hear crates and cages being knocked over off camera, and the sound of broken glass.

This would have been around seven-o'clock. Jack had gotten a visit from the police at a quarter to nine.

He'd actually sent Chuck and Lindsey home early that day, getting ahead of the storm. Jack, himself, had been riding it out off-grid. He'd gotten home to discover his phone missing from his pocket, probably left absentmindedly on his desk at work, and so he never got the security alarm once the fire-sprinklers went off.

The police and fire-crew had arrived at the Institute to put out the fire only to discover a parking lot full of cobras and vipers retreating from the flames. One fireman was nearly bitten before the Chief ordered them back.

Officers Benton and Lewis were on the scene, and both knew Jack. When he didn't answer his phone, they sent a car directly over to pick him up.

When Jack arrived, the fire was already out, just from the overhead sprinklers.

The surrounding parking lot was bare. Any retreating critters had vanished into the surrounding fields.

Jack looked at the propped-open doors. He wondered what might still be roaming the halls. He glanced grimly at Officers Benton and Lewis, hefting his catch-bag and snake hook.

Cautiously, he ventured in the front entrance. The halls were still misty with smoke, but the fire was restricted almost entirely to the Venom Lab.

The floor was empty, obviously most of the animals that had escaped, dogs, monkeys, had all already abandoned the building. He would still have to be careful in the corners, though – a lot of the bugs might still be crawling around.

As Jack made his way to the Venom Lab, he found those doors propped open as well.

On the floor inside, he saw three bodies, all black-garbed and masked.

Moving one-step at a time, Jack made his way through the lab, deliberately uprighting every overturned crate and cage.

There were several cages still in place – all the lance-heads, thank God – but pretty much everything that had been knocked over was empty. Everything that *could* get out, was already gone.

Jack called in Benton and Lewis.

Officer Benton had nodded when he bent over the first dead body, pulling off the man's mask.

“Yep,” Benton said, “We've seen this guy before. He's always starting a fire somewhere.”

“One of James Warden's disciples?”

Benton nodded.

Jensen unmasked the other two. A young man and a woman.

“Seen both these two, as well. They usually specialize in campus protests.”

“Well,” Jack sighed, “I guess we're affiliated.”

Then he had recognized the face of the young woman. He'd seen her in protest marches too. When she showed up, the news always made a point of singling her out. Now Jack kneeled beside her still-cooling corpse, looking up at the two officers.

“Don't you realize who this is? It isn't just some random street-activist. This is Elizabeth Williams.”

Benton and Jensen exchanged glances. They knew George Williams.

Among other things, that meant the situation had just gone from serious to high-profile.

Officer Benton peered inside a couple of the unopened cages. A big lance-headed viper took umbrage, posturing up in the strike pose behind its glass.

“Jesus,” Benton whispered, turning to regard all the other broken, empty cages. “What exactly crawled out of here tonight?”

Jack shut his eyes, running down an extremely unpleasant checklist.

Then he looked out into the dark, open fields surrounding the Institute and all the wooded areas behind, and tried to make an honest assessment.

The 'bugs' were probably still close, and a lot of them probably hadn't even made it out of the building. The scorpions were the worst of those.

There *were*, however, those big Japanese hornets. They had range. They weren't the one-shot killers that a death-stalker was, unless you were particularly sensitive, but they were also a risk to potentially breed.

The spiders weren't *too* bad. Even the worst of them weren't in the scorpion's league, but some of the big Mygalomorph 'tarantula' breeds, were fast runners, and might cover distance more quickly. The funnel-webs and the Brazilian wandering-spiders were the most dangerous on that roster, and just like the hornets, they could breed in the area just fine.

But except maybe for the flying hornets, none of the other bugs should be a great risk to the wider public.

The escaped snakes were another story.

Jack had seen both mamba cages broken and empty. And the taipan. Almost all the cobras, including the king. Most of the exotic vipers like the African Gaboon and puff-adders, and the Latin lance-heads were still in their cages. But almost all the rattlers were gone – the eastern and western diamondbacks, the Mojaves, the Cascabels.

He would have to go over their inventory to get a final count, but Jack guessed at least thirty getaways.

"What crawled out of here?" Jack repeated. "The absolute worst of the worst."

And in the days that followed, that phrase was repeated in the press. In this instance, Jack was happy to let all the local yellow journalists be as salacious and gore-crow as they wished, because he *wanted* people scared. Leslie Daniels and her cronies were at least good for that.

There was also pontificating from city hall on 'cracking down' on over-the-top acting-out from people claiming to be protesters. That was no doubt at the immediate behest of Mr. George Williams. And whether it materialized into something substantial, the incident did bring an uncharacteristically negative public reaction in James Warden's direction – the obvious suspect – and angry online comments on his own blog even accused him of coordinating a deliberate Manson-like effort.

Jack broke it down more simply than that. On top, there was the dumb-ass factor. The break-in was obviously bungled sufficiently for the damn fools to end up dead. And there was the old saying that incompetence can look like malfeasance, so can dumb-ass look like evil.

But Jack had another one too. The road to Hell was paved with good intentions. Historically, righteousness quite often *far* exceeded the atrocities of intentional evil, because whether you were talking Inquisition or enforced eugenics, it wasn't much more than virtue-signaling 'till it hurt.

The problem with do-gooders, was that they never stopped. They had the courage of their convictions. And if sometimes there was a Holocaust, or a mass slaughter, well, they *meant* well.

This was where Jack put people like Liz Williams, who everyone that knew her said was a wonderful person.

It was a natural enough pattern. After all, if you read the Bible, ultimate evil was nothing but corrupted virtue. What was Lucifer but a fallen angel?

Of course, that assumed the virtue was there in the first place.

Jack wasn't sure that was really the case with James Warden. Because there was another hidden-level under all that affected piety. And that was the simple appetite for destruction.

What evil lurks in the hearts of men? Just waiting to be released?

And what better permission than a good cause?

Jack wondered if the public would buy it this time.

So far, the city had made no official statement, but the comments on James Warden's blog were increasingly inflammatory.

'The Warden' was not accustomed to public ire, particularly in the Willamette area, but this time people were dead – three of his local recruits, one a popular student at the university with important political-ties. He'd been thrust into deeper water than he'd expected.

Seeming to sense the unfavorable opinion-shift, he made a brief statement on his blog, the day after the break-in.

Normally, after any of 'The Warden's' operations, this was where he would be bugling, but this was a deliberately vague, solemn epitaph, bemoaning the regretful deaths of all three, praising their courage and dedication, singling-out 'medical-student Elizabeth Williams' most of all – and carefully denying any direct ties.

In point of fact, Jack had been told by Officer Benton that specifically connecting him to the break-in was what the city was waiting on.

“It actually shouldn't take long,” Benton said. “Warden's pretty brazen with his methods. Any texts or emails he sent are probably right there on his phone.”

And Jack had no doubt those texts were there. He wondered what the city would ultimately do, but in his own humble opinion, just for the break-in alone, James Warden should be looking at manslaughter charges, at the very least, Liz Williams' political-ties notwithstanding.

But now the reports of what happened to the Connors family were going public.

After two-weeks of ambivalent silence, the city announced a warrant for James Warden's arrest.

CHAPTER 8

With the Expo coming up Saturday, there were going to be a lot more venomous snakes coming to town.

They had been planning a big one this year, ironically, at least in part to counteract all the negative publicity.

The Expo was reptiles in general, but there was always a particular focus on 'hot-herps'. The Institute's presence provided the air of authority. Not only did it have a muting effect on any illegal transactions that might otherwise be going on in the background – the University was, after all, a state institution – it was also a safe-place environment for owners to offload pets that might have become too much for them.

Jack had actually not worried overmuch about Florida's problem with invasive-exotics occurring locally. The Everglades were practically a preserve, supporting everything from invasive pythons, to monitor lizards, to pigs, that were all running rampant over the already endangered local ecology. There were breeding populations of cobras, possibly even kings, and a garden worker working at a house bordering the 'glades was bitten and nearly killed by a green mamba.

After the break-in, however, a little quick revisionist review caused him to reconsider the local habitat. While your taipan or mamba was not acclimated to the Northwest like your average garter, snakes could be hardy, surviving in the damnedest places. Reptiles in general would surprise you that way. There was an alligator found living on the Applegate River in southern Oregon, near Grant's Pass, in 2009, probably a released pet. Another was found in someone's driveway.

With that in mind, there was no reason to think some of these other escapees couldn't at least survive, even if they weren't actively breeding.

Jack was at least glad Dean Brown was letting the Institute keep a presence at the Expo, for the purpose of adoption. After all the advance publicity, there would probably be an even larger than normal turnout of adoptees, so it might even work out better that they not waste the time or manpower on a booth, which was really just public relations. This way, they would simply post a sign at the gate, sending drop-offs to the back, and spend all day processing them without distractions.

It would also allow them to stay discreet.

Jack understood that was a priority now. In practical reality, he begrudgingly agreed, but the thought of it burned him. It amounted to complete capitulation, after all, allowing thuggish tactics to prevail.

Still, he understood that any more disruption would only keep him from doing his own job, and too few people seemed to understand that meant saving a lot of potential lives.

The fact was, Jack actually considered the standing death-toll of eight, counting the three at the break-in, making only a total of two incidents, very damn lucky. So the last thing Jack wanted was more trouble.

He hoped they could just get through the weekend without incident.

Alas, such was not to be the case.

They would not, in fact, make it through the following day.

CHAPTER 9

Right up to the moment he found the Connors family dead, Jack had actually been entertaining doubtful hope that they might yet avoid any dangerous encounters between the public and the remaining runaways.

That luck, it seemed, had run cold. There were three more incidents on Friday.

The first involved a Cascabel, *Crotalus durissus,* an extremely bad-tempered Central and South American rattlesnake, approaching diamondback-size, with one of the most toxic venoms among pit-vipers.

Kids had been playing soccer in a field, and a sixth-grader had nearly run right over the top of it. The young boy, whose name was Tommy Doyle, said later he thought it was an old car-tire, and didn't hear the rattle until it was too late. He was hit with both fangs in the leg.

He had been running, so he actually pulled past and away quickly, but the snake's nearly inch-long fangs had both penetrated.

Tommy screamed, stopping the game immediately, and parents had come running – wisely avoiding the still-coiling, and posturing rattler, giving the five-foot snake ground like a potentially-spreading fire, they rushed the kid to the hospital, bypassing the ambulance, and just taking-off in a speeding caravan of mom-vans.

Meanwhile, almost five-miles away, completely on the other side of the surrounding neighborhoods, another young mother – whose own kid was actually *at* that same soccer game with his father – came out to her backyard, to find out what her little dog was barking at.

She found the little pooch lying on its side, gasping, whining and whimpering, seemingly unable to move.

Frightened, the woman had bent to help and an Asian cobra reared-up out of her landscaping.

She had frozen in shock and the thing bit her on her arm and leg.

This time it was neighbors, alerted by her screams, who came to the rescue, spiriting her off to the same hospital.

Fortunately, in both cases, the staff was ready with the appropriate antivenin. Janice was the direct liaison to the hospital to make sure the species involved were correctly identified, and treatment for both patients was prompt on arrival.

The woman with the cobra-bite, Mrs. Donna Campbell, suffered difficulty breathing but was turned around quickly by the antivenin. There was minor swelling – cobra-venom tended towards neurotoxin, but some Asian subspecies, depending on the geography, showed acidic hemotoxic effects as well, especially among those breeds known to spit. In the case of Mrs. Campbell, once the venom passed, she was mostly good as new.

It was a nearer thing with Tommy Doyle and the Cascabel-bite. The snake hadn't gotten him with its full-load, but it would have been a fatal dose for a kid his size, if not for the prompt treatment with antivenin.

Cascabels were unique among rattlesnakes with neurotoxic qualities to their venom, actually painless, as opposed to the tissue-destroying hemotoxin in most other rattlers. Its bite caused paralysis and death from respiratory failure, although renal failure and blindness could also occur.

Young Tommy went briefly blind, and stopped breathing. Only the fact that he was at the hospital within minutes saved his life, getting him on a ventilator until antivenin could be administered. But once the effects were neutralized, he came around quickly. He was kept overnight as a precaution, but expected to make a full recovery.

Of course, that still left the recalcitrant serpents at large. After Janice sent him news of the bites, Jack texted Chuck and Lindsey, sending them both after the Cascabel, while he went after the cobra.

Chuck and Lindsey's little foray went fairly smoothly. The big rattler was still out in the middle of the soccer-field and easy to spot, having made no particular effort to hide. The two of them, with snake-hooks, rounded-up the five-foot rattler just fine.

The cobra had decided to make a run for it. Jack searched Donna Campbell's entire yard, finding nothing, until there was a sudden screech from behind the fence, two yards over.

He vaulted the fence, sprinting across the neighbor's backyard – eliciting a brief, barking objection from the dog lying on the porch – before climbing over the gate to find a woman pulling her young daughter up into her arms and fleeing up onto the back porch.

She saw Jack and pointed.

"It's a cobra!" she cried shrilly. "It's right there."

Jack hopped into the yard, zeroing in, and spotting the slithering movement behind the rose bushes. He glanced back at the mother.

"Are either of you bit?"

She shook her head.

"It just stood-up in front of my daughter while she was playing in the yard. I pulled her away."

Jack nodded.

"Stay inside," he said. "I got this."

The cobra was moving along the fence behind the flower-bed, looking for an opening to slide through. Jack caught its tail with the hook, pulling it out into the grass, where it reared-up to face him. He turned his catch-bag open, using the hook to simply lift the four-foot snake bodily into the bag and twisting it shut.

Behind him, the mother was recording the episode with her phone.

“This is going on my social-page,” she told him. “You're my new hero.”

Jack smiled. That was a better reaction than he'd been used to lately.

Both culprit serpents, now captured, were thus returned to the Institute.

Jack went home that night thinking that, all-told, they had been quite lucky once again.

It was with the third incident that day when that luck, such as it was, ran the rest of the way out.

This time, it involved another black mamba, the missing male.

Four dead – and among them, Dean Herman Brown and his son Bradley.

CHAPTER 10

What happened to Dean Brown and his family was no accident. The mamba was delivered in a package by a private courier.

It was a simple packing box, roughly the size of a small suitcase, and its return-label was the university's sports department.

Young Bradley Brown, living at home during the summer before his last eligible year on the team, had accepted the package, and opened it on the dining room table.

The male mamba had been coiled inside, ten-feet long, curled like a garden-hose in the cramped space. It had likely been jostled about during transit, and the air-holes poked into the sides were deliberately small, so as not to be obvious.

It left the snake extremely testy. The moment Brad cut the strapping tape and opened the top, that mamba popped out like a Jack-in-the-box.

The Browns were affluent. They had security cameras in the main rooms and walkways of their house, and this was all recorded clearly.

Brad took three strikes in the face, almost instantaneously. Security footage recorded his startled, "Oh *shit!!*" as he stumbled back.

The snake got him once more on the hand as it sprang out of its box, slithering out onto the dining-room floor, where it postured-up defensively against the wall.

Brad was backing away towards the stairway, looking down at his hands, and then touching the bite-spots on his face.

This time when he spoke, his voice was slurred.

“Oh *no...*”

Then he collapsed.

He knocked over an end-table as he fell. The crash brought his parents and little sister from the family room upstairs. They found Brad paralyzed and not breathing.

His mother, who worked as a volunteer nurse at the university hospital, had bent to administer CPR and nearly stepped-on the still-testy mamba, who had made an attempt to hide under the table. But now confronted with three more lumbering house-apes, the snake lashed-out angrily.

Herman Brown had pulled out his phone, evidently intending to call for an ambulance, but now he turned to see his wife hit with several strikes, before the tiny, black mouth flashed in his direction too. He took three bites, in the leg and stomach.

Brad's little sister, Amy, an aspiring nurse herself, moved to intercept the snake, and she also took several hits, all in the face and arms. She looked down at her hands, disbelievingly, and then, like her brother, simply collapsed.

The snake retreated back under the table as the last of its antagonists fell. The cameras recorded no more movement from the family. Coroner reports estimated they were all dead within minutes.

They were discovered early that evening by Herman Brown's older sister, coming by for dinner, who found them lying as they had fallen.

CHAPTER 11

Jack went home that night ready to be done with it all. When he sat down in front of the TV, today's two lucky survivors were being profiled on the news. To her credit, Leslie Daniels was letting them tell most of it, and at least in the case of the eleven-year-old soccer-player, she wasn't gore-crowing it as much as Jack might have expected.

She, of course, made up for it once the TV switched to footage of Jack himself, taken in previous years at the Expo, along with a segment filmed at the Institute.

Jack remembered the day Leslie Daniels and her crew came to the Venom Lab. Uncomfortable in front of a camera, Jack was finally persuaded by Dean Herman Brown himself, into submitting to the interview. Good PR, he was told.

So Jack had showed the film-crew all the scary ones – the Gaboon viper with its hyper-long fangs, the giant king cobra, and of course the mamba, tapping its cage enough to make it pop up, showing its ebony-black mouth.

For the venom-milking demonstration, he chose one of the Asian cobras – small enough to control, what with the added risk of people in the room, but also a good visual, as it reared up and showed its archetypal cobra hood and the double-eye markings on the back.

Jack remembered the cobra made a quick move off the tongs when he pulled it out of its cage, and he had caught it deftly, expertly, by the tail. The movement sparked a brief screech from the film crew, which was audible on the final edit. But as he now sat back in his chair, watching the sequence on TV, Jack took note of his own on-camera poker-face.

He remembered that moment well, and watching it on television, you would never know the unconscious chill that sparked up his spine every time his skin touched dry, rough snake-scales.

You couldn't see it in the video, but the doubling back always brought him back to the first moment he had ever felt that smooth, tactile roughness sliding across his bare skin.

Jack's own '*got-bit*' story – the one at secondhand.

He had been eleven-years-old. He'd been out camping with his older brother David, and one of his friends, over David's strenuous objection. Forced compliance won the day, and David, four-years older, was operating under direct orders from their father.

Still, it had been a pleasantly rowdy night. David and his friend, a nice enough kid named Robbie, hadn't really minded having Jack along. They made a small fire around a rocky clearing near the lake, toasted marshmallows and franks, smoked a couple of stolen cigarettes and drank a couple of pilfered beers, ate beans, told lies, joked, and farted all night – a perfect forum of sophomoric wit, and for Jack, as a tween-age kid, it was the sanctum sanctorum – his first night out with the big kids.

They'd stayed up late and fallen asleep in their sleeping bags under the stars.

Jack woke some indeterminate time later.

Something had roused him. In the fuzziness of sleep, the first thing his eyes focused on was the moon. In dreamy, momentary confusion, he began to stir.

That was when he heard the rattling. And became aware of the weight upon his chest.

In the crackling of the firelight, he could see the coiled rattler, looking him in the eye, poised not three-inches from his face.

Jack's breath stopped, locked in paralysis, as he stared back, frozen motionless in his sleeping bag.

Then he felt something moving in the bag with him.

In another moment, a second rattler poked its head out, and Jack felt the flicker of its tongue on his cheek. Then he felt the smooth scales as it slid up and over his face and neck.

Silently, he began to cry, lying there unmoving, tears leaking. He couldn't hear either of his camp-mates. But he couldn't cry out. He lay too terrified to breathe.

In fact, he lay there for almost twelve hours before his dad found him... and the bodies of David and Robbie. Both of them had been bitten in the night.

The snakes were long gone. To this day, Jack had no idea when they might have finally left.

And to this day, there was not one moment when that interminable night was not just a little bit with him.

Nor was the memory ever far of attending his brother's funeral, and then his friend, Robbie's, a few days later.

He often wondered when they had died, while he lay paralyzed and helpless.

The memories always brought personal guilt and shame, worse than terror or grief.

Jack felt very much like that now, as he watched the news, with Leslie Daniels tearing open some of his more recent wounds. And with what had to be deliberately-edited cause-and-effect sequencing, they showed the mug-shot of his arrest, directly before running a slideshow of all the recent dead – including high school photos of the vandals from the original break-in, and highlighting "popular local med-student, Elizabeth Williams."

The messaging wasn't subtle. Jack knew the actual facts, but it worked on him too. Somehow, it *felt* like it was all his fault.

Exhausted, with such dark thoughts and images on his mind, Jack began to doze. And then he began to dream.

It was the sort of dream where you knew it was a dream. And he'd had it enough to know what was coming.

Sure enough, the couch in his living room was somehow transformed out on the campsite again, and once again, he could feel the slide of snake-scales across his bare neck.

In his soupy, subconscious semi-awareness, he lay still and waited, because with his adult educated herpetologist's mind, he knew that's what you were supposed to do.

Jack had actually seen the truth of that clearly demonstrated. Years after the incident in the campsite, while pursuing his degree, he witnessed a 'snake-sitting' by a researcher named Austin Stevens, who lived in a glass cage with some sixty-odd venomous snakes, including mambas and cobras, for a period of weeks.

Stevens had been interviewed, and Jack remembered him laughing as he described sleeping in the cage, with a black mamba's cool form sliding across his neck.

At the time he first heard that, Jack excused himself to the lavatory and puked. He'd had the dream that night as well.

Tonight's version was fairly typical. The variation was that he was still sitting in his recliner out at the campsite, but that sort of thing always made sense in a dream. The pertinent focus was always the slide of snake-skin against his bare neck. Having been through it so many times before, he did what he always did – he lay still and waited for it all to play out again.

These recurring somnolent-vignettes were mostly about the nighttime – that long stretch before he even thought to wonder about his brother or his friend. It was never about the part after the real waiting started, as he still lay there the next morning, once the sun got hot, and he began to believe he was going to die.

Jack stirred a little in his chair, still afraid to move in his dream, but twitching back to wakefulness.

He blinked and he now saw his TV screen instead of the old campsite. The news coverage had ended. Leslie Daniels was gone and the station had moved on to weather and traffic, entering into the dinner-hour. Outside, the sun hung deep on the horizon, and the small rented house was shaded and dark. Snippets of dream played tricks with the shadows.

In the soupy blurriness of sleep, Jack focused on movement in front of the screen.

As his eyes cleared, he realized he was looking at a mamba reared up in front of his chair, its black mouth gaping open.

Jack gasped, belatedly remembering all those stories about them stealing into native huts in Africa, leaving whole families dead.

Just like the Connors.

Jack froze, but the mamba darted forward anyway, right into his face.

Then there was a loud knocking, and Jack sat up in his chair.

He looked around, shaking off the last of the dream. In defense of the nightmare-phantom mamba, he had tossed the remote in his hand across the room.

Then he heard another loud knocking, and Jack realized that was what woke him. Someone was pounding hard on his door.

“Doctor Wright?” an authoritative voice announced. “If you're in there, we need you to open up. This is the police.”

CHAPTER 12

It was Officers Hammond and Cates who picked Jack up. Benton and Jensen were waiting outside when they arrived at Dean Herman Brown's house. The yard was cordoned off, and the paramedics stood at bay, waiting on Jack.

They had ventured inside long enough to ascertain everyone was dead, but on Benton's call, they were waiting to remove the bodies until Jack gave them the okay.

There were fewer neighbors gathered outside than at the Conners' house. Dean Brown lived in a higher-end neighborhood, much more spacious and spread-out.

It was also clear on the other side of town. There was no way the mamba had crawled all the way out here from the Institute. And when Jack found the open-package, he realized what must have happened.

Things had taken an even darker turn. Jack hadn't thought that possible.

It seemed 'The Warden' had taken things to the next level.

Payback for jail-time? Jack wondered. Or perhaps just simple escalation? Maybe it was just personal over the fist-fight at the coffee-shop.

Security cameras mounted in the kitchen and living room would fill in details, but Jack could see how it played out clearly enough. He picked up the empty shipping-box.

Their male mamba was ten feet long. He couldn't imagine it had been cooperative going in.

And where did they find the damn thing? Just happenstance? Jack had been hunting for it in the bushes for a couple of weeks.

He at least hoped it was still in the house.

But a quick search only took a few minutes to round it up. The mamba hadn't gone far, retreating into the laundry room, coiled-up under the sink.

Jack got lucky this time. The dryer was running, creating vibrations, hiding the soft thump of his footsteps, and the snake remained unaware until he got in close.

He caught the mamba behind the neck with his snake hook, pinning it to the ground and getting a quick grip on it before it could offer any meaningful response. Pulling his catch-bag around, he turned it over the snake's head, flipping the bag over the top, and tumbling the ten-foot length of coils inside.

Deftly, he dropped the mamba's head and twisted the catch-bag shut.

Jack's heart took an abbreviated beat, that moment of relief he felt every time he performed this simple move, where a misstep could mean his life.

He took a breath, holding the bag at-length.

Inside, the mamba was thrashing belatedly. Jack could see the fangs poking through the bag, staining the cloth yellow with dripping venom.

Officer Benton was waiting at the door.

"You got it? Is that the only one?"

Jack nodded, indicating the torn shipping box.

"It looks like someone had it delivered."

Jack held up the bag with the squirming mamba inside.

"That means someone not only caught this thing, but boxed it up and sent it across town without getting themselves or the courier killed."

Benton shrugged.

"Any particular suspects?"

They both knew the obvious. But this was a level up in vicious, even for the likes of James Warden. There were also a couple of practical realities to consider.

"Well," Jack said, "I'd say you were looking at an experienced snake-handler, except that sometimes idiots can do incredibly stupid things and still not die."

Benton nodded, waving to Jensen and the waiting paramedics, who started unloading their stretchers. Out on the street, a few more neighbors were gathering.

Jack took his catch-bag to his car, folding it carefully inside the trunk.

When he looked up, he saw a flashy convertible Mustang pulling up beside the ambulance.

Lindsey was already stepping out, almost before the car was parked.

She was poised as if to run for the door, but then she saw Jack, just closing his trunk, with the catch-bag inside. As if in a trance, she began to walk towards the house.

Officers Hammond and Cates moved to intercept her, but Jack stepped forward quickly, waving them off.

He took Lindsey by the shoulders, meeting her eye.

She already knew what he had to say.

"They're all dead?" she asked.

Jack said nothing. He just nodded.

There were a few moments of sheer blankness, an utter vacant response as Lindsey absorbed this.

In those moments, another vehicle turned down the street, pulling to an urgent stop.

No emergency van, this time, Leslie Daniels and her news-crew piled-out like kids at recess.

Lindsey was still registering, blinking repetitively, like a computer processing too much data, too fast, but the look of impending grief in her eyes was briefly replaced by the cringe of apprehensive dread, reflexively covering her face, as if in anticipation of the blinding lights and cameras.

Then her eyes turned back to the house. The paramedics were bringing out the first stretcher – just in time for the news-crew.

This would be Bradley Brown, popular quarterback, Lindsey's presumed 'not-quite' fiancé.

Now her face broke. Jack held her and she cried into his arms.

Behind them, Leslie Daniels' cameras recorded it all.

CHAPTER 13

James Warden was arrested later that same night.

Jack and Lindsey had just arrived back at the Institute, and Jack was just unloading the mamba in its catch-bag from his trunk, when Chuck appeared at the building's door. Jack had sent him in to inventory their Cascabel and Asian cobra serum, and he had been watching it all on the break-room TV. His eyes turned doubtfully to Lindsey, his face somber.

"They got him," Chuck said. "James Warden's in jail."

He held the door open anxiously, and they followed him inside. In the break-room, the TV was blaring Leslie Daniels and the local news.

The Brown house was onscreen, surrounded by flashing lights. They managed to catch Jack on camera again as well, this time catching Lindsey too, weeping into Jack's arms. The shot was just too dramatic not to exploit.

Chuck glanced over at Lindsey.

"Are you okay?"

Lindsey was still in the very early stages of acceptance, looking a bit shell-shocked, with all the implications still sinking in – not just the *fact* that Bradley was just suddenly gone, but it was apparently a deliberate murder.

With all this not yet fully absorbed, Lindsey simply nodded robotically, the appropriate social response to be acted-out. Chuck glanced worriedly at Jack, who shook his head with a shrug.

Chuck turned to the TV that was now showing a past mugshot of James Warden, and the camera crew was standing outside a rather ratty-looking apartment building.

"They apparently got him on an anonymous tip," Chuck said. "He was living in some local flophouse under an assumed name. I don't even think it was that he was hiding. That's just how he lived."

"Where did he get the snake?" Jack asked.

Chuck half-laughed, shaking his head.

"Well, they *think* he was keeping it in a box under his bed."

Jack blanched, remembering the torn-open shipping-box.

"In a cardboard box? Under his bed for almost two weeks?"

Chuck nodded to the TV. Leslie Daniels, who seemed to be operating on Red Bulls tonight, had one of James Warden's quad-mates on-camera, being interviewed.

"They had this guy on earlier. He was looking a little green at the thought. Apparently, they share a wall."

Jack wondered if this was the tipster. He certainly seemed wide-eyed enough. Outraged too, and not afraid to say so to Leslie Daniels.

"That idiot could have killed every one of us in the house."

Jack was actually relieved to see the anger. James Warden had always been above-reproach when it came to the moral high-ground. But behavior had consequences. For people in that neighborhood to call the police required a significant grievance. Discovering your roommate was keeping a deadly snake in a loosely-sealed box just on the other side of your wall was certainly cause enough.

To be fair, James Warden would not be the first to pull that sort of thing. The field was ripe with stories of owners being careless, or even flat-stupid with hot-herps. Jack heard of a kid who'd bought a Gaboon viper illegally, and was hiding it in a shoe-box in his underwear drawer, with a note on top – '*Mom, venomous snake, do not open*' – which his mother did, although fortunately the tepid Gaboon had just lain there.

That would not be the case with a high-strung, active mamba.

As if responding to the thought, the snake, still hanging in its catch-bag tossed in its confinement. Lindsey glanced over, and now her pale stoic expression cracked just a little, suppressing an involuntary shudder. Jack nodded and turned to put the mamba away, sliding it carefully out of its bag into its own cage right next to the female's.

Lindsey turned away, briefly, as if blocking a moment of escaping emotion from breaking through.

At the very least, today's events would not help her phobia over handling the mambas. As it stood, both the male and female in their charge had together killed nine people.

Dealing with her grief was going to be something else. Because Jack knew it was a little more complicated than it appeared on the surface.

Chuck, eager to be sympathetic, lay a comforting hand on her shoulder. Lindsey tolerated the physical contact, although Jack saw the wary glance of a pretty girl.

Perhaps seeing it too, Chuck pulled back quickly. Jack hoped the kid wouldn't try and use today as a lever to wheedle his way in, while Lindsey was bereaved and vulnerable.

But Chuck simply stepped back, pulling on his pack, donning the helmet he now wore for riding the motor-scooter he'd bought now that mass transit was too hazardous.

"I'm headed home," he said, nodding to Lindsey. "Call me if you need to talk."

Lindsey smiled politely, accepting one more brief hug.

After Chuck let himself out, Jack turned to Lindsey.

"Why don't you stay home tomorrow," he suggested.

Lindsey smiled, slumping in her chair, glancing after Chuck, as if she'd been waiting for him to leave.

"I'll come in," she said. "I need to stay busy."

"You don't need to be distracted," Jack warned.

Lindsey shook her head.

"I won't be. I'll be focused."

Jack eyed her carefully. He had a high opinion of her, so he was inclined to take her at her word. This job was about nothing if not keeping focused under pressure.

Still, he knew she was factually under extra stress. He debated simply ordering her to stay home.

At that moment, his phone beeped. Jack looked down, seeing Janice' name blinking an incoming text.

"*We need to talk*," it said.

Jack tapped back: "*I'm at the Institute*."

Janice messaged back promptly: "*Already on my way*."

Jack pocketed his phone, turning to Lindsey, who was gathering up her purse.

"Are you going to be okay tonight?" Jack asked.

Lindsey held up her own phone.

"My Mom's already sent a dozen messages. My sisters too. And my friends." She smiled reassuringly. "I'm not alone."

Then, abruptly, she began to cry again.

The torrent was as sudden as it was severe, seeming to fold in on herself, as if just saying it brought everything home at once.

Uncertainly, Jack pulled her in, once again holding her until the storm passed and she finally sat back.

"I'm sorry," she said. "It's just that with everyone calling me... I don't know exactly how to feel. And I'm scared I feel differently than everybody thinks I should."

She knew Jack remembered their conversation just a few weeks ago. Now she hung her head like in a confessional, because he was the only one who really knew.

"I was going to break it off with him," Lindsey said. "I'd been chicken-shitting out for too long, and I'd finally made up my mind. I was going to talk to him this weekend."

She glanced up, furtively, looking for judgment.

"Now?" she said. "Everyone expects me to be grieving. And I *am*. It's just..."

She covered her eyes reflexively, as if with shame.

"Everyone feels so sorry for me because I lost him. But I was going to leave him. Only I can't say that to anyone. So it's like I'm lying about what I actually lost. And I just feel so guilty. So phony."

Her face broke briefly once again, and she fought it back.

"Then I remember he's dead, and that I'm just feeling sorry for myself, and I know everyone will hate me."

She was holding back her tears more successfully now, but Jack gave her a reassuring hand on the shoulder anyway, making sure to keep it proper.

"Honestly," Jack said, "there's nothing for you to feel guilty over. I would just accept the consolation and smile."

Lindsey smiled, touching his hand, and then leaned into a big deep hug, utterly unaffected, just filling the need of physical human comfort.

Jack smiled, hugging her back. This was why he liked Lindsey – just simply being real. With another girl, it might have *been* inappropriate.

Of course, it certainly looked that way when Janice walked in, her phone in her hand, but stopping on a dime as she saw the two of them embraced.

Jack caught the look in her eye over Lindsey's shoulder, and stood away. Lindsey glanced back, wiping off running make-up.

"Bit of a personal loss today," Jack said simply. A safe enough statement, and it pertained to all of them.

Janice was Herman Brown's second at the university, and while no one had said it yet, that meant she was now acting Dean. The issue might be decided at length upon review of the university board, but for the moment, she was next in line. Going forward, all the decisions would be hers.

"Lindsey," Janice said, "why don't you go on home for the day. I'd like to talk with Jack privately."

Lindsey glanced at Jack, who shrugged.

"You'll be okay," he told her.

She held up her phone and all the blinking messages from Mom, friends, and sisters, and she smiled painfully. She nodded a good night to Janice as she let herself out the door.

On TV, Jack's face was back onscreen. Now his mugshot was side-by-side with James Warden.

"There have been arrests on both sides," Leslie Daniels' voice-over intoned.

This was immediately followed by footage of Mrs. Robins, taken just the other day, demanding accountability and that arrests be made.

Janice frowned, turning off the TV.

"That's it," she said. "Things are too hot. I'm shutting this place down."

CHAPTER 14

"I thought we were already shutting down," Jack said.

Janice nodded.

"I mean right now. I don't want you or your staff coming in tomorrow. You especially."

Jack frowned.

"Why? Am I a liability now?"

"No," Janice replied immediately. "You're too hot. I'm worried about you getting hurt. Or even getting in trouble trying to defend yourself. Isn't that what happened last time?"

She eyed him.

"And yes, I'm worried something is more likely to happen if you're here."

Jack said nothing, debating whether to be more frustrated or angry.

"Look," Janice said, "Go out in the field tomorrow, for one last sweep. We've got a few outstanding getaways left. The king, the taipan, among others. See if you can't round-up a couple more of those. Anything you catch you can deliver directly to the Expo."

Jack eyed her, catching the implication, but making her say it.

Janice sighed, and gave him the rest.

"I'm also taking over at the Expo. I'll be handling everything there myself."

Jack shut his eyes. Frustrated was winning.

"Your face is too public," Janice said. "I'm just trying to avoid trouble."

"So am I," Jack said. "If someone comes in with something sketchy, you'll need me there."

Janice nodded. She'd heard the horror stories. Her favorite was the mamba in the pillowcase.

"I'll be fine," she said. "Once the show is over, I'll ship everything off to Idaho tomorrow night."

She eyed him.

"I don't suppose you'd be willing to go along?" she asked. "See things on the other side?"

Janice shrugged.

"There's no real need for you to come back. I can finish things up here."

Jack nodded.

"Get rid of me once and for all?"

Janice looked crestfallen.

"Jack," she protested, "it really isn't like that. But let's face it, sticking around is just asking for trouble."

That, Jack had to admit, was undoubtedly true. And there was a certain attraction to simply tossing off and leaving it all behind. He had been planning to go anyway.

"Jack," Janice said, "for what it's worth, I'm sorry it all ended this way." She paused, as if debating her words. "I... think you're a really good guy. I always did."

Janice was looking at him earnestly. For a moment, Jack felt the impulse to explain his visually-compromising pose with Lindsey when she'd walked in, but decided that would only make him look self-conscious.

As he was getting older, the realist was overcoming the idealist and he was learning the value of just shutting-up. Why not just bring up the whole '*Jump-your-bones-McCoy*' thing?

"For what it's worth," Jack said, "I'm *really* sorry about the whole '*Jump-your-bones-McCoy*' thing."

Janice smiled.

"I'm sorry my boyfriend beat you up over it. To be fair, that whole night was mostly my fault. But I was drunk and you were a good kisser."

Jack smiled.

"Well," he said, "I might not be seeing you again for a while."

His grin grew just a bit cheeky.

"Wanna hug?" he asked, spreading his arms.

Janice politely extended her hand for a shake. Then, when he took it, she smiled and pulled him in for a hug.

"Keep in touch," she said. "I'll take care of everything here."

Jack went home for the night intending to let her do just that.

The Expo was tomorrow. Off to Idaho when it was over.

That meant an early morning. Their window had closed, and they only had one more day to find the remaining getaways. Not to mention that mamba-nest.

Although as it turned out, they didn't even have that.

CHAPTER 15

There was actually a fourth incident that day, although no one would know about it until the following Monday.

The lost taipan had been lying low, somewhat under the radar. The species was a bit overshadowed by the publicity traditionally granted the black mamba, but *Oxyuranus scutellatus,* the coastal taipan, was, in fact, the number-one pick by many experts as the deadliest serpent on the globe. It was more toxic dose-for-dose than the mamba, with a bit uglier list of symptoms, adding blood-coagulation and arterial-hemorrhaging to the neurotoxic-effects, and like its African cousin, it boasted a fast-acting venom that hovered right near a hundred-percent fatality-rate without treatment.

The taipan from the Institute was a large, healthy male, over seven-feet long, and it had made its way to the first of the rural houses north of the highway, where people owned a little livestock. The family that lived there was the Jacobis. Two parents, and two teenage daughters.

Police were later able to piece together the unfortunate sequence of events. There were no living witnesses.

It wasn't even really a farm – just a big, plantation-style house, with a shed and a few chickens.

And it was that chicken-coop that attracted the snake.

In fact, the taipan made itself right at home, slipping in and helping itself to one of the hens, before curling up under the comfortable solar-heated cages.

The other hens, of course, had objected strenuously, attracting the attention of the Jacobi's youngest daughter, Tina, who went out to investigate.

She'd expected to find a coyote or maybe a raccoon. But all she saw was one of the coops empty. She didn't see the snake coiled below it, until it struck her three times.

Tina had shrieked, stumbling back and tripping, falling to the floor, whereupon the snake struck her three more times in the face.

Six bites from a taipan would pretty much be a death-sentence for a full-grown elephant. Tina weighed a hundred-and-ten pounds. She collapsed almost immediately.

Next was her sister Lori, finally coming to look after her when the caterwauling from the chickens didn't stop. She found her little sister sprawled on the floorboards.

When she bent over her, the taipan hit her twice in the face as well.

And as police later determined, the rest of the family went the same way. The mother, June Jacobi, had likewise gone to investigate, finding both her daughters lying stone-still. And just as Lori had, bent her face down almost right in front of the increasingly testy snake.

Charles Jacobi arrived home from work to find an empty house. When he, himself, had gone out to the chicken-coop, his wife was lying in the doorway.

She was still alive, and he had bent over her, checking her breathing, preparing to administer CPR. Then he had seen his two daughters.

He was reaching for his phone when the taipan came out from under the coop once again, evidently having had enough disturbance for the day. It shot for the door, but Charles Jacobi was in the way – although when he saw the hissing snake lurching at him, he did his best to move aside.

Not quite enough – the taipan hit him in the leg. Charles tripped and fell back, tossing his phone. The angry snake bit him twice more in the stomach and butt, as he rolled. Then it shot for the fence.

Charles Jacobi started crawling for his phone. He made it about halfway.

The Jacobis wouldn't be discovered until the following Monday. By then, the events at the Expo would already be national news.

CHAPTER 16

As per Janice' instructions, Jack texted Chuck and Lindsey to meet him at his place in the morning instead of the Institute, with a brief explanation.

Chuck had replied with a frowny-face, and a brief, "*Got it*".

Lindsey's emoji-face had a tear on its cheek.

"*Does this mean you're leaving after tomorrow?*"

"*I will probably drive over with the shipment tomorrow night*," he sent back.

She sent two teary-faces back.

They all met at Jack's little rented house at eight the next morning. As he waited for his team, drinking his coffee, he got an early morning text from Janice.

"*Just got news*," it said, "*James Warden has been released.*"

Jack blinked at the message. Even though his inner-cynic should have expected it, he still found himself blindsided. That was literally overnight. Janice had sent him a link to the news report, and another text, "*Call when you're up.*"

He tapped her number. Janice answered on the first ring.

"Jack? You saw the story?"

"Just the headline. What happened?"

"All they're saying at the city is that they have evidence exonerating him."

"What, exactly?"

"You now know as much as I do."

Jack growled silently to himself.

"You think there might be trouble at the Expo?" he asked.

"Well," Janice said, "We've got a restraining order against him, and he's got priors now."

"So *after* he does something dangerous, he might get in trouble for it? I'm not exactly encouraged. Even if he doesn't show himself, he's got a lot of disciples."

Janice sighed.

"Well," she acknowledged, "he's already encouraging it online. He's playing it like his release is an exoneration for everything else. And now it's time... and I'm quoting directly here, 'for some true accountability.'"

Jack did not particularly like the sound of that.

"Janice," he said. "Seriously. Now I'm concerned for *your* safety. Maybe you should just call it off today. Any drop-offs at the Expo will just have to take their snakes back home this year."

"I'm already here," Janice said. "I'm going to stick around as long as things stay cool. This is a city-facility, after all. It's a little too public for them to be acting-out too much."

"Is that what recent events have led you to believe?"

Janice hung on her reply.

"Point taken," she said. "Where are you right now?"

"I'm at home, waiting on Chuck and Lindsey. We're going to take one more day in the field. Our count is down to a dozen unaccounted for. Plus a few bugs."

"Okay," Janice agreed. "Keep in touch."

As he was tapping his phone off, he looked up to see Lindsey's Mustang pull into his driveway. Chuck was sitting in the passenger seat, head bent, frowning unhappily at his phone, no doubt already reading the news about James Warden's release. Chuck still had a divot in his scalp from a swinging skateboard.

Jack opened his front door, stepping out, sealing the lid on his coffee-thermos, as he waved a morning greeting.

"You heard?" Lindsey said, nodding as she climbed out of her car.

Her face was worried, but deliberately calm. It was her cobra-face, Jack thought. Anxious, but in control.

Still sitting in the passenger seat, reading his phone, Chuck looked angry. Shaking his head, he tapped the screen off and clambered out of the car.

"They just updated the news report online," he announced, his tone exasperated. "The reason they let James Warden go is because they have footage of someone else delivering the mamba package to the courier."

Jack frowned. "Who?"

"No I.D., but apparently someone obviously a lot smaller. Probably a kid. He's wearing a hoodie with a hat and glasses. Wore gloves. Prints on the box are all from the courier's staff."

Jack sighed bitterly, wondering if that was Addy Robins again. Or it could have been any number of acolytes. Warden would have to be an idiot to deliver the package himself.

But apparently that amounted to the perfect crime to the Silver Lake, PD.

Or probably, more likely, the city-council and the local D.A.. Jack wondered briefly what Officers Benton and Jensen thought about it.

Although, if everything went according to current plan, he would probably never see either of them again to ask. He would be leaving tonight. Once the Expo was over, he would simply throw his suitcase in his car and follow the delivery truck all the way into Idaho. Janice had agreed for the university to pick-up a motel-tab until he found an apartment.

And then he would be gone.

He glanced at his two interns, who were looking back at him unhappily. As far as he knew, neither of them had any immediate alternative career-options on the table. Chuck had only gotten his internship in the first place because Jack had interceded. He would have to speak to Janice about repositioning both of them somewhere further down the trough. She'd been making an effort to make this all painless, so he was optimistic she would be receptive.

Hopefully, that would at least take care of *his* people.

But he was a little more worried about the mess he was leaving behind. Until Janice' little announcement last night, Jack had actually been considering staying in town past the Institute's closure, and simply continuing the hunt. There was nothing that said he, as a private citizen, couldn't go out and hunt cobras and vipers all on his own.

The real issue was, could he, in good conscience, walk away from the situation, knowing the likelihood of someone, not just being hurt, but killed, was pretty high?

But now the decision was being made for him. An entire shipment of hot-herps being delivered on the fly, merited his full attention. His greater responsibility lay there, and he would have to let the city deal with the remainder of the escapees. He hoped Janice, at least, would be given a hand in assigning personnel to handle the last of the round-up. There were many professionals like himself she would know, who could take care of it competently enough, who didn't have their faces broadcast on Leslie Daniels' mug-shot reel.

Chuck and Lindsey were eyeing Jack expectantly. He shrugged.

"Well," he said. "You know the score. This is our last day on the job. The Institute is basically closed now. Janice doesn't want any of us anywhere near. That has to go double now that Warden's back out. Any runaways you catch, take them directly to the Expo."

Jack shrugged, and extended his hand to Chuck.

"Well, kid," he said, "It's been good working with you. Good luck in your career. I expect you to do well."

Chuck grinned, a touch sadly.

"Thanks, Jack," he said, shaking his hand. "And thanks for all your help over the years. It's meant a lot."

Jack turned to Lindsey, who tapped her eye, like her sad-face tear-icon. Jack smiled.

"Well, Scarecrow," he said, "I think I'll miss you most of all."

He extended his hand. She pulled it in for a hug, kissing him on the cheek.

"I'll miss you too," she said, stepping back. "Thanks for being a friend last night."

It was actually a nice moment – interrupted abruptly by the flash of blue lights. Jack turned, blinking, blinded briefly, as a police car turned into his driveway, directly behind Lindsey's Mustang.

They were considerate of the neighbors, and refrained from sounding their siren. It was Officers Benton and Jensen who got out of the car. They looked apologetic.

"Hey there, Jack," Benton said, coming up the front walk, nodding to Chuck, and smiling appreciatively to Lindsey. "Sorry, to bother you this morning, but..."

Benton stopped, glancing back at Jensen, as if pained to say it.

"We've got to place you under arrest," Benton said. "Apparently that Mrs. Robins bitch..." he grunted, glancing at Jensen who shrugged. "Mrs. Robins has been raising all kinds of hell downtown. She's got a whole squad of other neighborhood mothers demanding that the Institute, and you in particular, be held responsible for the deaths caused by the escaped animals."

"She's also got the D.A. taking another look at your altercation with her underage son, and calling it a prior," Jensen added.

Jack frowned. That might be more indicative that people like George Williams were listening to her too.

"Let me get this straight," he said. "You just let James Warden go, but *I'm* being taken to jail."

Benton nodded with a humorless, affirmative smile.

"And just so you know," he said, "Mrs. Robins has also been talking to the press. That's why we decided to pick you up early, before you got to work. If we can get you in and processed, we can duck you past Leslie Daniels and her pack."

Jack supposed that was considerate.

Otherwise at a loss, he turned to Chuck and Lindsey who were both watching, wide-eyed.

"Well," Jack ventured doubtfully, "I will apparently be otherwise occupied today. I guess you guys go ahead as planned."

"I'll call Janice," Lindsey said, "and tell her what's happened."

Jack smiled, nodding, and extended his hands to Officer Benton, who produced a pair of handcuffs, and with an apologetic look on his face, latched them around his wrists.

"Sorry about this, Jack," he said.

Jensen held the cruiser door for him as Jack was helped into the back seat, and taken into custody.

CHAPTER 17

Janice was standing at the expo-center's main backroom freight door, when she heard the mob walking up the street.

And yes, she would qualify it as a mob.

There were security-screens mounted on the wall next to the door over the freight-receiving desk, and the camera-view was set to the front parking lot. Janice watched the rest unfold on her phone, once the day's events broke into the morning news.

She had told Jack she would be careful, and intended to bail if things started getting hairy. But once it all started happening, she wondered if she would be able to.

It was still early, but the reptile-expo was open. Visitors were already wandering past the booths. The main crowd usually started arriving around nine, and would last until the show closed at five.

The plan after that was to load-up whatever donations/adoptions came in. They had a big trailer truck backed right up to the rear dock. Once that was full, back to the Institute one last time, load-up that inventory, then it was off to Idaho and the new facilities waiting there.

Unfortunately, Jack's arrest threw a kink into that plan. He was supposed to oversee the transfer on the other end. This was hazardous cargo to say the least, and they needed an expert on hand.

Janice considered Chuck and Lindsey. They could go on the university's dime. But there was administrative bullshit needing doing too, and they were just two kids good at snake-handling.

She could go herself, except she was now the new head of the university, on extremely short notice.

Not that leaving this particular shit-storm behind wasn't attractive.

But she also had to deal with Jack's arrest.

The fact of it was only starting to really sink in. In the short term, she had determined to focus first on her duties at the Expo. Jack always said, distraction is not allowed in this trade.

Janice was less of a handler than Jack, or really, even Chuck or Lindsey. She was a scientist, whose hands-on skills were the sort of competence you have after a lifetime interest, based on a belief of minimal contact. That is to say, she could catch and bag a snake, but wasn't into the day-to-day handling required for, say, milking venom.

But she did have experience with a wide variety of reptiles, including the odd python, or even monitor lizard or gator.

And there were all kinds at the Expo this year. The hype had been big, and the local troubles with herps only fanned the publicity. Janice was actually surprised at the early crowd. And as they wandered the aisles, the exotic fair didn't disappoint.

Janice walked all the displays while they were setting up that morning. There were breeders, pet-shops, even wholesalers, some selling hatchlings in fairly large volume, all lined in glass jars. Of course, most display booths boasted terrariums containing grown adults, a menagerie from all over the world.

Cobras were always popular, particularly the Asian cobras, *Naja naja*, with its classic double-eyed pattern on his hood, quick to rear and spread, and famous for dancing to the snake-charmer's flute. It was also notorious as one of the 'big four' venomous snakes, racking the highest death-toll worldwide.

There were also a lot of African cobras. In fact, her first adoption of the day was an Egyptian cobra, *Naja haje*, the 'asp' that killed Cleopatra. The man who brought her in said it almost got him too.

A college-age guy, who Janice recognized as the Fraternity-type, had laughed, showing his bandaged hand. Apparently, the snake clipped his finger while he was cleaning its cage.

The young man, who introduced himself as Dave, had driven himself to the hospital, not feeling any symptoms, and was never administered antivenin.

"It was either a dry-bite," he said, "or the blood washed the venom out."

Janice favored a dry-bite. Cobras were known to do that in self-defense. A lot of snakes, elapids and vipers alike, would dry-bite, although some were more generous about it than others. Taipans would envenomate nearly eighty-percent of the time. And, of course, the black mamba was pretty much every single time.

You heard words like '*a hundred percent*' a lot with black mambas.

But even with the cobra, fraternity Dave was extremely lucky. He lived in northern California. A serious envenomation, especially having driven *himself* to the hospital, could have very easily been fatal before any antivenin could have reached him.

He did, at least, seem to have learned his lesson, first in bringing the snake in for adoption, and second, in the no-expense-spared travel crate, with the snake cage inside it – *two* layers of security.

Once bitten, twice shy, as they say.

The Expo also had a lot of 'spitters' this year, all secured behind glass. There was the Mozambique spitting cobra, *Naja mossambica,* and the ebony-black

Ringhal – taxonomically not a 'true' cobra, but a closely related genus, *Hemachatus haemachatus*.

A surprise adoption this morning had been a large king cobra.

The donor was a woman Janice recognized from previous years. She was a gypsy-type belly-dancer, who called herself Lola, and performed with snakes. In the past, she'd brought in mostly pythons and boas, as they grew too large for her act.

The king was a personal pet, which she was giving up for the same reason – it was getting too damn big.

And king cobras could attain fairly imposing size. They were recorded up to eighteen-feet, and Janice guessed Lola's snake was easily over fifteen. Snake-catchers had mistaken kings for pythons. And it was intimidating as all hell when a cobra reared-up tall enough to look you in the eye.

King cobras were another separate genus, *Ophiophagus hannah* – 'snake-eater' – a reflection of its diet, which consisted almost exclusively of other snakes. As such, its venom was adapted to be more toxic to reptiles than mammals, like humans.

Despite its reputation, the king was also actually a fairly congenial serpent temperament-wise. They were handled almost casually in some localized cultures in Asia, even by children.

On the other hand, they were known to aggressively defend nests – the only snake to do so. And while they were commonly known to 'dry-bite', when they *did* envenomate, their size allowed them to release a flood of venom, many times a fatal-dose, and it was a toxin that, like the mamba and the taipan, could get you in trouble quickly.

Janice had seen at least two other kings on display today. They were good for photographs, usually willing to rear-up and spread their hood behind the glass.

There weren't many rattlesnakes this year. That had been a developing trend over the last few Expos. Rattlers were a bit prosaic, being native to the region. It was the exotic species that people were interested in, and would travel to come and see.

On the viper-front, there was a full assortment of Central American vipers on display. And besides all the Bothrops lance-head genus, from *B. atrox* and *B. asper,* to *B. lanceolatus,* out on the floor, Janice had been donated one very large bushmaster.

The bushmaster, *Lachesis muta,* was the king cobra of vipers, up to eleven-feet with a heavy viper-build, giant fangs. It was possessed of a fearful reputation, even though it was responsible for few deaths in the deep jungles were it lived.

Its mortality was high, however, upwards of eighty-percent, and there was a saying in the region: '*If a bushmaster bites you, go and sit down beneath a tree, because in a few minutes you will be dead.*'

The man who brought it in was another repeat customer Janice had known for years, a longtime collector named Robert Walters, a PhD doctorate like herself, who was getting older, and had been paring down his collection over the past several years.

"My reflexes aren't what they used to be," he confided to Janice. "Getting old sucks, but I'd like to *keep* getting older."

Walters had also brought in a common krait.

These were a particular species that gave Janice the creeps, and it was primarily because they looked so ordinary.

Kraits were a little off-the-radar, in terms of notoriety, but in truth they were another one of the 'big four'. Where the black mamba was the '*seven-step*' snake, the common krait, *Bungarus caeruleus,* was the '*one-step, two-step*' snake for the same reason – that was all you got.

They were generally inoffensive by nature, but were night-hunters, pursuing rodents, often into village huts. A serious envenomation from a krait had a fifty-percent fatality-rate, even with antivenin, because the toxin caused respiratory paralysis that was irreversible, putting victims on ventilators until they simply died.

Kraits were elapids, cobra-relatives, but the snake coiled up in Walters' little carrier looked as docile and inoffensive as a loose bicycle tire. That was what always got Janice – they didn't even look mean like a cobra, or a rattler, or scary like that black mamba-mouth – they were almost a little bit cute.

But if it bit you, fifty-fifty survival was your *best* chance.

Another underrated attendee at this year's Expo was the boomslang.

One of the larger booths, run by an amateur enthusiast named Bernie Wright, a collector who specialized in African species, kept several boomslangs. *Dispholidus typus*, a primitive rear-fanged serpent related to garter snakes – a Colubridae species, that boasted among the most toxic, drop-for-drop venom known, but was once actually thought to be harmless, because it lacked the hypodermic-injection mechanism of other, more advanced front-fanged snakes.

Of course, his most prominently-featured exhibits were the African mambas. Bernie's collection had all three species of green mamba – the western, *Dendroaspis viridis*, the eastern, *D. angusticeps*, and the Jameson's mamba, *D. jamesoni.*

The green mambas were smaller, and their venom was not as toxic, but they were extremely agile tree-dwellers, and their venom was likewise fast-acting.

They were also nervous and prone to strike without much provocation.

But the crown of Bernie's collection – and anyone's, really – was their notorious black cousin, *D. polylepis*. Bernie had two, both in the same cage, right up front for the passing public. Both snakes were happy to oblige the visitors with open-mouthed threat-displays behind the glass, perfect for pictures, and Wrighton's booth typically drew a crowd.

On a normal day, Janice could walk these aisles for hours, studying every booth, and every cage. She would never get bored with it.

But today, she was apprehensive. She wanted this Expo over and done.

With Jack already sitting in jail, and the warnings from Officers Cates and Hammond, Janice stood her post in the back, taking donations as they came in.

She was just beginning to hope things might actually be okay.

Then right about nine o'clock, at just the time when the parking lot was starting to fill-up and cars on the main through-way were slowing down and lining-up before the turn into the expo-center, the first of the protesters made their appearance.

You could hear the crowd chanting before they became visible, marching purposefully up the street.

CHAPTER 18

The crowd coming up the street was flooding into the main lot, blocking off anyone who wanted to leave by car.

Mrs. Robins was at the head of the crowd, holding a sign that read '*Accountability Now!*', surrounded by others that said, "*Arrest and Prosecute!*'.

There were two wheelchairs being pushed along. In one of them, was the woman who'd been bitten by the Asian cobra. Mrs. Donna Campbell. Janice remembered her name from the hospital that day. Rolling next to her, being pushed by his mother, was Tommy Doyle, the sixth-grade soccer-player who'd taken the bite from the Cascabel. A couple of the other neighborhood mothers walked with them. Susan Burnett, who'd appeared on the news after her kids had seen a mamba in their backyard.

Janice did not see Mrs. Robins' skateboard-wielding son, Addy – at least, not at the front of the crowd. Perhaps the optics would have been a little too ironic.

Or probably more likely, the kid was up to dirt somewhere else. Janice just hoped it wasn't anywhere close.

The police had anticipated trouble. When Officers Hammond and Cates met her at the back lot early that morning, they told her there was already buzz about a protest on social media.

That was also when they informed her Jack had been arrested. She'd gotten a text from Lindsey bare minutes later, telling her the same thing.

Janice was still processing all of this, but this last news had changed her mind about a lot of things in a hurry.

The fact that the city was actually going after Jack was now giving Janice pause about continuing her own position at the university. She never wanted to be an administrator. In fact, she'd only accepted the position as number two because it seemed like a promotion. And it *was*, for paychecks, but it took her out of the research part. At the time, she thought it would have looked bad career-wise to turn it down, but now, having literally been handed the head-job, her first impulse was actually to turn in her resignation.

She was already quietly angry over the city's acquiescence to what she frankly regarded as thugs. And as a lifelong academic herself, she'd encountered the odd *'Mrs. Robins'*, with her unwavering, and even haughty defense of a son who could have very easily killed one of the members of Janice' own staff.

In fact, that very statement might be included in her resignation letter, perhaps even one best given after calling a press-conference in order to say it all publicly. It occurred to her that, acting as the current university-head, she actually had the power to do that now.

And as she regarded the mob forming in the parking lot, blocking people from coming in, but more importantly, coming *out*, Janice decided that, whether she decided to keep this job or not, a press-conference to deal with that very subject, up to and including Jack's arrest, was going to happen Monday-goddamn-morning.

They still, however, had to get through the day.

Officers Hammond and Cates had parked right next to the main entry-gate. The two expo-security guards, a pair of pay-by-the-hour hominids who were introduced as Brooks and Palmer, were pulled-up behind them in their expo-center security-van, attempting to look official, but they remained rooted in their seats, as the crowd approached.

When the protesters moved to block the street, Officers Hammond and Cates beeped their siren briefly and flashed their lights, rolling their cruiser forward into the road, parting the crowd.

Amiably, both policemen stepped out of the car, waving people back to the curb.

"Out of the road, folks," Hammond was saying. Both he and Cates were big men, and a lot of the crowd was local moms.

But not all of them were. Janice saw many Addy-clones. And worse, more than a few full-grown doppelgangers of James Warden.

The crowd wasn't pushing back at the two cops – at least not yet. But now they lined up along the main drive, holding up their signs – not *quite* in the road, but close enough to intimidate traffic.

From inside, a number of Expo-visitors had come out to see about the commotion. Others were still arriving, and both were immediately subject to hoots and catcalls.

And while Officers Cates and Hammond facilitated traffic control, at least allowing cars *in*, they did nothing to disperse the crowd.

Mrs. Robins began leading periodic chants, with different rhyming combinations, but all pretty much demanding '*accountability*'.

Janice was still not a hundred-percent sure exactly *what* they were demonstrating over. The Reptile-Expo was not attached to the Institute, beyond its typical yearly booth and its snake-adoption program. At the moment, Janice herself was the only university-employee in the building. The expo-center's connection to any escaped snakes, or any altercations with James Warden, was minimal.

On the other hand, they *had* been pumping the promotion up this year, so it could simply be free-association. Or perhaps they were taking advantage of the public event to shout into cameras.

Then, as if things couldn't get worse fast enough, Janice saw Leslie Daniels' news van pulling up into the main lot, parking behind the security van beside Cates and Hammond's cruiser.

Leslie and her crew filed out, cameras and lights already on. Seeing her moment onstage, Mrs. Robins started up another chant, holding up their signs – 'Children have DIED'.

Dutifully, Leslie Daniels turned her camera on the protest, inserting herself in camera view, taking background footage as they prepared to go on the air.

There was a beep from Janice' phone, a text sent from the expo-center administrator, who had retreated to his upstairs office. He was a cantankerous old country fellow named Ron Wilson, and the Reptile-Expo was already not his favorite gig of the year. He was a farmer first, used to handling livestock and running the occasional rodeo. His biggest security-deals were usually the concerts that sometimes played the venue.

Wilson had already been told by Officers Hammond and Cates that the police presence was only in case the demonstration got violent.

"So," Wilson had reported back to Janice, "the plan is apparently to let this loud angry mob threaten and harass staff and visitors, and if they get riled-up enough to get violent, all *two* of those cops are gonna put the kibosh on it."

Expressing little confidence with this plan, Wilson had retreated to his office upstairs, trying to get somebody from the city to answer their phone, text, or email. His latest text to Janice read: '*No luck.*'

Currently, Officers Cates and Hammond simply stood in front of their cruiser, where it sat by the gate next to the security guard van – both guards remained in their vehicle. Cates and Hammond smiled and waved amiably, both at incoming and leaving guests, as well as the sign-waving protesters.

Hopefully, just their presence would deter too much acting-out.

For her part, Janice stayed in back, out of sight, watching it all unfold on the security cameras and the news-feed on her phone.

She didn't know how much of this was about the Institute's responsibility in the recent deaths, versus James Warden's network acting out his personal vendettas. Neither did she know how much her own face was tied to either one.

In any case, there was no sense pushing her luck. Trying to leave might risk being recognized, so for the moment, she stayed where she was.

Meanwhile, outside in the parking lot, Leslie Daniels was now interviewing the protesters. Up first, was young Tommy Doyle in his wheelchair, with his grave, on-the-verge-of-tears mother standing behind him.

Janice groaned as Leslie made sure to focus in on the soccer ball in his lap, as she zoomed in on his still-bandaged leg.

"Your son," she was asking his mother, "was bitten by an exotic snake you had no idea was being kept less than a mile from where you lived?"

A rhetorical question, but Mrs. Doyle nodded, losing the battle with her tears.

"I think how close we came to losing him," she said, through hiccupping chokes, "and he was just out playing with his friends."

Next was cobra victim Donna Campbell, whose own son walked beside her wheelchair, carrying a picture of their family dog.

"Ringo was Timmy's pet," Donna said. "He was already almost dead when I found him. It could have been me."

Janice felt bad about the dog. On the other hand, she knew Donna Campbell had *walked* out of the hospital after her cobra-bite, and probably did not need the visual-aid of the wheelchair.

And in both cases, it was antivenin created and promptly provided by the Institute that saved her and Tommy Doyle's lives.

Next up, Mrs. Janelle Robins.

This was not the first time Leslie had spoken with Mrs. Robins, so she knew what to expect. Rather than asking questions, she simply extended the microphone and let her go.

It was actually fascinating to watch. And convincing too. Mrs. Robins' outrage did not seem affected at all. Janice wondered how much really was consciously deliberate, and how much was utterly unaffected blind rationalization.

Janice had to hand it to her – the woman knew how to maximize her air-time. In sixty-words or less, she bounced quickly from the 'assault on her son', to the 'deaths of families and children', making sure to name-drop 'that poor girl, Elizabeth Williams', and holding the Institute responsible for all of it.

To Leslie Daniels' credit, or perhaps just out of her own confusion, she took a moment to question this last point.

"The Reptile-Expo has nothing to do with the Institute," she said. "Or the University. Why protest here?"

Mrs. Robins crooked her head scornfully.

"Leslie," she said, as she would to one of the seventh-graders in her class, "you know perfectly well that the Willamette Institute, this unethical, vivisectionist torture chamber, has been directly involved with this dangerous event for years."

Mrs. Robins' hands were on her hips, leaning forward.

"Now you go in there and tell me if you don't see the very head of the Institute, the very head of the university, in there right now."

Well, Janice thought glumly, watching the broadcast, it looked like she was on the radar after all. And if they'd found out she was here, Janice wondered if they knew she was here alone.

Onscreen, Mrs. Robins was pulling another one of the mothers in front of the camera. Janice recognized the woman with the cobra in her yard – the one Jack had snared, before she or her daughter had been bitten. The woman's name was Wendy Squires, and she had been on the news just yesterday, shaken by the incident and gushingly thankful to Jack.

But today, her tone had changed.

"At first, I was grateful," Mrs. Squires told Leslie Daniels, "but now I think how close my daughter came to being bitten by that thing." She nodded to Mrs. Robins. "Janelle here, says that's like thanking a drunk-driver who pulls you out of a burning car, after he drives you off the road."

Janice' face darkened. That was a pretty hardcore spin.

She was still quietly absorbing the simple fact that Jack had actually been taken to jail this morning. Being so busy, she'd not been able to give it her full attention yet, and so had not yet been truly alarmed.

But with rhetoric like *that* being tossed around, Jack's arrest just took a more serious turn. The sheer absurdity of it had kept her from appreciating the full implications.

Causes were big in this city. It was why people ran for office, and those who were elected wielded their power that way, because a noble cause always provided the automatic moral high-ground.

And to demonstrate all that morality, you had to go after '*bad guys*' every once in a while. You just had to be clear who the local public perceived as 'bad guys'.

This was a city that released James Warden, who was positively connected to the initial break-in, but had taken Jack into custody.

It actually looked like a sacrifice on the altar of public opinion.

And ironically, perversely, based on comments online, James Warden's release had turned around the initial negativity he'd been getting since the break-in. The perception now was evidently that, because the police couldn't prove he sent the mamba to Dean Brown's house, this somehow absolved him of his direct attachment to the release of the mamba and the entire venomous cast still crawling around at that very moment.

Yet Jack's arrest seemed directly related to his own responsibility, and by extension, the Institute's responsibility for their safekeeping. It apparently shouldn't have been so easy to break-in and let all those deadly snakes out.

If the city actually intended to pursue something like manslaughter charges, or even wrongful death, for... how many dead, so far?... Jack could be looking at twenty-years-to-life in prison.

And that was assuming they stopped there. Janice, herself, was head of the Institute and now head of the University itself, and if they were ultimately judged responsible, criminal circumvention of security, notwithstanding...

Well, *she* was an even bigger fish than Jack.

Onscreen, Leslie Daniels was asking Mrs. Robins about Dean Brown, recently killed by a snake deliberately sent to his home. Mrs. Robins' comment was telling.

"I would say," she said, looking at the camera directly, "some chickens came home to roost in a big way."

Out along the main walkway, catcalls were starting to go back and forth between the protest-line and the mid-morning crowd arriving for the Expo. People drove slowly past the signs, some looking hesitant, some aloof, a couple exchanging fingers.

One of those erupted into a scuffle as the arriving guest added a few catcalls of his own back at the crowd – broken-up quickly by Officers Cates and Hammond, who sent both combatants on their way. Perhaps under orders, the security-guards, Palmer and Baker, still hadn't gotten out of their seats.

But now someone on the protest-line threw a rock into the parking-lot. There was the crash of a broken windshield.

Janice watched this all, dry-mouthed. Leslie Daniels' cameras had turned to the scuffle, but the sound of breaking glass was audible. You could hear Officer Cates talking into his radio.

"Okay," he was saying, "it's kicking-up a notch."

There was a static reply, to which, Cates responded, "They're getting rough, and the city doesn't want us getting rough back."

Within five-minutes, Administrator Wilson's voice came over the expo-center's intercom system.

"I'm sorry, folks," he announced in his country-drawl, "but I just got word from the city that this event is being closed down, for reasons of public safety. Please retain your tickets and they will be refunded or exchanged for future events."

And then, with a note of concern, "I deeply apologize to everyone, but you all saw what's happening outside. As you leave, please do not engage any of the protesters. We have police on-hand, but we don't want any trouble, and we don't want anyone hurt."

That actually started a murmur through the open hall.

The intercom beeped.

"Once again," Wilson said, before switching off, "I'm very sorry."

Janice couldn't believe it. She was outraged.

So the thugs just win? What were you supposed to do when the adults-in-the-room just indulged the tantrum?

She almost tapped Wilson's number, but realized that was futile. This clearly wasn't his call.

Janice threw up her hands. To hell with it. She would send out an announcement that donations were closing down, and then she would start securing the freight load of hot-herps for transport. Once everything at the Expo was done, back to the Institute, load-up their stock there, and send the truck off to Idaho.

As she'd been working over the logistics in the back of her mind, she was leaning towards sending Chuck and Lindsey to oversee the shipment, and Janice would simply try to supervise where necessary over the phone.

She needed to turn her attention to Jack, sitting in jail, and figure out what she could do about it.

Janice turned to the rear dock, where the semi-trailer was backed-in. She'd already been loading the donated serpents on board, meticulously making certain each was safely secured. She would take anything anybody brought out in the next few minutes. And then she would simply hang out back here until the Expo was officially shut-down, and both the visitors and the protesters were gone.

Then her eye caught movement at the back door. Janice turned to see three figures, all dressed in black, come running up.

They were carrying bottles with burning rags stuffed in the spout – makeshift bombs.

Janice recognized one of them as Addy Robins.

They threw their burning Molotov-cocktails into the warehouse.

The first two broke against the wall and doorway leading out to the main expo-hall. Flame began spreading immediately.

But the one Addy threw broke against the cab of the semi, igniting the gas-tank, and it exploded.

CHAPTER 19

Chuck and Lindsey were on the trail of the king cobra. They could tell by the tracks, because this particular getaway was the largest snake in the Institute, both longer and heavier than their bushmaster. It was nearly sixteen-feet long and forty pounds.

Lindsey was always particularly cautious with elapids, because they were more likely to break Jack's 'range rule' than a viper that struck out of a circled coil, most often pulling back after a strike. An elapid moved its whole body forward.

Cobras weren't as bad as the Australian elapids, like the taipans, or God-forbid, the African mambas, because they tended to rear-up and fall forward. But their attack was straight on, and if they were being aggressive, they would sometimes come right at you.

The king cobra was generally an inoffensive snake, known to dry-bite more often than not. Lindsey had seen video of Indian villages with literal toddlers handling kings, pushing them bodily out of the way as they crawled past their crib.

Of course, they did get temperamental defending their nests. And like any animal, you could always provoke it, like say, by trying to catch one, just as they were doing now.

When it chose, the king cobra was potentially the most formidable snake of *all* – viper, cobra, *or* constrictor. Besides being one of the select few snakes capable of killing elephants, the name 'king' came from the fact that it actually *ate* other snakes, including all but the very largest pythons.

Its title, as it turned out, was well-deserved, even in Silver Lake.

Chuck had been tossing the brush a few yards ahead, and just turned the path when he stopped dead.

"Oh my God, Lindsey," he said. "You have *got* to see this."

Lindsey hurried up beside him, her snake-hook ready.

In the little clearing, was the king, and it wasn't alone.

It had the taipan by the neck. Both snakes were entangled, but the cobra was over twice the size of the Australian elapid – the third most venomous in the world, and a close contender with the black mamba for science-consensus deadliest.

Today it was lunch. Janice had seen the way kings operated – they would simply sidle up to the other snake, and grab it by the neck, as supple as a mongoose. That fast-acting venom, which could drop a full-grown pachyderm, would have killed the taipan in seconds.

Even as they watched, the tangle of the two snakes seemed to unravel as the taipan fell limp. The cobra held its jaws locked nonetheless, making sure.

Chuck had his phone out, filming the scene.

"Oh *this* is going viral," he said.

Lindsey wasn't listening. She was slipping into her game-face, moving with focus. That was necessary on a normal day, let alone after the last two.

She was deliberately, consciously aware of her own stress-levels. On top of everything else, she was still freshly-reeling from the scene with the police taking Jack off to jail. And that was after an entire night of calls from her mother, sisters, girlfriends. She was still getting texts and emails from well-wishers.

Lindsey had basically decided to take Jack's advice – accept it and smile.

Still, she was exhausted today. The walk in the woods had actually been therapeutic, Chuck's nattering notwithstanding.

Lindsey obviously recognized Chuck's crush, and tried to be nice about it, while simultaneously not encouraging it, and preserving the gentle fiction that it didn't exist.

She could tell he wanted to be comforting, though. He'd sent her a feeler first thing this morning.

"Are you going to be alright?" he'd asked hesitantly. "About Brad?"

"I'm fine," she said briefly. She'd had enough bereavement counseling overnight to last her.

Chuck pushed just a little.

"I mean, I only ask because you don't want to be distracted out here."

"I *won't* be," she said, a touch curtly. "Actually, I'd rather not talk about it."

"You talked about it with Jack..." he began, but then stopped.

"I'm sorry," he said, "I'm just worried about you. I hope you're okay. I think you're a good person and I'm sorry this happened to you."

Lindsey thanked him, neutrally, and they had both turned their attention to today's last snake-hunt – one that actually seemed to be bearing a pair of ripe fruits.

Now Chuck was focused completely on the chase. He liked cobras, but especially kings. You cage them together, even a black mamba would be eaten in short order.

Currently the big cobra was working itself into position to swallow the still-twitching taipan.

"Should we let it eat?" Lindsey asked. "It might be easier to catch if it's full and slow."

Chuck nodded, edging closer, getting a better angle on his phone-screen.

"That might not be a bad idea," he agreed. "I want to get this on camera anyway."

But the movement was a mistake, the snake saw it as a threat.

Suddenly, it reared, dropping the dead taipan, and standing-up, hood flared, nearly in Chuck's face.

"Oh *shit*," he blurted, stumbling back, dropping his phone, but the cobra was moving forward.

At sixteen-feet long, it could rear Chuck's own height. He raised his hook to ward off the incoming strike, but it was already going for his face.

It would have got him too, if Lindsey hadn't snatched it by the tail, yanking it back, bare-inches from Chuck's face.

The big cobra curled back upon itself, its mouth gaping, fangs ready to inject a full-load of venom. There would be no dry-biting here today.

And king cobra venom worked fast.

But Lindsey expertly guided the snake's body, hand-over-hand, keeping tension on the tail, tossing the snake's own weight back at the head, always warding it off and away.

Recovering his wits, and blinking as he realized how close it had been, Chuck moved quickly forward and caught the cobra around the neck with his own hook, just as it twisted back again, trying to strike at Lindsey.

With two hooks together, they were able to stretch the snake out. Chuck pinned it to the ground with his hook, even as it was now trying to run. But Lindsey still had it by the tail.

Chuck stepped forward, grabbing the pinned snake by the back of the head. He let go of the hook with his other hand and grabbed hold of the cobra's neck. Lindsey did likewise, controlling the big king's writhing body.

"Well," Chuck said. "That got my attention."

Together they wrestled the cobra into a catch-bag. Chuck twisted the top shut, holding it on the end of the pole, away from his body. Lindsey hooked the dead taipan, wary lest it suddenly inexplicably revive, and tossed it into a separate catch-bag.

Chuck looked after the dead snake regretfully.

"It's unfortunate we couldn't get it alive," he said. "That was a valuable animal."

He bent to where he'd dropped his phone. The camera was still recording but the screen was a cracked spider-web. Chuck muttered a curse, but shrugged.

"Oh well," he said. "It's a good video anyway."

They spent twenty-minutes walking back to Lindsey's car. The Mustang was parked at the edge of the woodlot, this one bordering the local high school. A minor waterway split the field, and the brush grew thick, providing a little oasis just off the highway for all the local critters. There were enough prey items to attract at least two of their getaways.

Lindsey opened her trunk, laying the dead taipan inside. Chuck put the catch-bag with the cobra on top of it. Lindsey pulled out her phone.

Reflexively, she popped-up Jack's number, to tell him they got the taipan and the king, before remembering he was in jail. Instead she sent the text to Janice.

Chuck shut the trunk, looking up at Lindsey.

"Well," he said, "that was a lucky catch, the last day on the job."

Lindsey nodded. Getting the taipan, dead or alive, was a real score. That would save somebody's life, for sure.

"Last day," Chuck repeated wistfully. "I guess we're not going to be seeing each other much anymore. I'll miss working with you."

Now, he looked humble.

"You probably saved my life today," he said. "A bite in the face would have been bad. Seriously, I want to thank you."

Lindsey smiled, allowing him to be vulnerable.

Clearly a mistake as, a moment later, he leaned in and kissed her.

For a moment, she was so startled, she actually let it happen. Then she pushed him roughly back.

He looked back at her wide-eyed.

"I'm sorry..." he began, but she stepped forward and slugged him.

Lindsey was taller than he was, as well as long-limbed and strong. She knocked him flat on his ass. He hit the gravel road on his back, blinking and holding his bleeding nose.

"God *damn* it," Lindsey exploded, standing over him threateningly. "Could you just try to be a *friend?*"

Chuck was sitting up, pinching his fingers over his nostrils. He looked up at her shamefaced.

"Sorry," he said.

Lindsey looked down at him with a slow burn. Then, with a disgruntled sigh, she extended her hand, helping him back to his feet. She had a first-aid kit in her back seat, and handed him a small hand-towel to douse the blood.

"Okay," she relented, "I'm sorry I hit you. And I'm sorry I don't feel that way about you. At *all.* Clear? I know that sucks, but I hope you can get past it."

She eyed him meaningfully, even as he daubed his bloody nose.

"I don't want to have to hit you again," she said.

Chuck pulled back the red-stained rag from his swelling-nose.

"Not a problem," he agreed.

Lindsey took out her phone again. Janice had not yet answered. She wondered how busy it was.

She tapped up the expo-site and got a news-bulletin across the top of her screen.

It took a moment for what she was seeing to fully sink in.

"Oh my God," she said, looking back at Chuck. "We've got to go."

At her tone, Chuck's attention turned from his nose.

"Why? What's happened?"

Lindsey was already moving around the car for the driver's seat.

"Big trouble," she said.

Chuck looked down at his own cracked phone, tapping and fiddling until the damaged screen brought up the news. He groaned aloud.

"Oh, those *idiots!*" he said.

Lindsey nodded, pointing to the passenger seat.

"Get in," she said, sliding behind the wheel, slipping her keys into the ignition.

Chuck was staring at his phone, frowning. He looked up at Lindsey as she started up the Mustang. Then, with a thoughtful expression on his face, he touched his damaged phone-screen, and began to tap out a text.

Lindsey was looking over her shoulder, exhorting him to get in. Chuck hit 'send', and then slid into the passenger seat beside her. Lindsey gunned the Mustang's engine, and squealed gravel as she pulled out onto the road.

She kicked-up dust, spinning tires, as they headed for town, leaving the small wooded oasis behind them.

And in the bushes, not ten-feet from where they'd been parked, but deftly hidden out of sight, in the grass running next to the creek, was a small nest of fourteen eggs, long, narrow and leathery.

The mother mamba had picked a good spot. So far, the nest had avoided crows, raccoons, and two snake-hunters.

So far, so good. All the incubating eggs needed was another six-weeks.

CHAPTER 20

Janice dived for cover a moment before the explosion, but she was still knocked unconscious.

She awoke in the semi-darkness of the back loading-dock, blinking and confused.

The power had been knocked off, but there was light from the open bay doors.

There was also light from the fire as the place burned.

Janice jerked up, sitting warily in the flickering half-light, smelling smoke.

The delivery truck was lying on its side.

No doubt a lot of its occupants had been killed in the blast.

But a lot of them were probably let loose as well.

And as Janice looked around, peering into the flame-licked shadows, the ground around her was *moving*.

She also heard the all-too-close sound of hissing – and rattling.

The rattling confused her for a moment. She hadn't taken any rattlers today. Then she remembered that big bushmaster. A lot of central and South American vipers used the tail-shake as a warning, whether they'd evolved a true rattle or not.

Janice stayed absolutely still until she spotted the big snake, coiled not six-feet away, reared-up in a striking pose, nearly as high as a cobra.

The big bushmaster was probably over ten-feet long. It could cover the strike-distance in a second. Janice remained unmoving, knowing her warm body stood out to the snake's pit-sensors.

That was the thing about pit-vipers – they could '*see*' you in the dark. It was one of the things Janice always found so fascinating about New World snakes – although right now seemed a lot more terrifying than interesting.

Bushmaster bites were extremely painful. And upwards of eighty-percent fatal. This one had her dead to rights.

The big snake eyed her, as if deciding whether to let her live. But then the fire seemed to make up its mind. The smoke and the heat were beginning to build up. The big bushmaster turned, stretching out of its coil, moving like a giant sidewinder for the loading-docks bay-door.

In fact, as the fire was now spreading quickly, the initial rush of escaped serpents, scattered in the aftermath of the blast, was now moving uniformly towards the exit and escape.

Janice rose warily to her feet, running off a tally of what she'd collected that morning. At least two-dozen hot-herps, less those killed in the blast, including a king cobra. Including kraits.

Behind her, the wall was on fire.

Now, she ran down a list of the deadly menagerie she'd walked past that morning. What, she wondered, might be the total count throughout the entire Expo?

Right now, all those cages were being kicked over, letting their occupants loose out onto the floor in the dark, right into a crowd in a burning warehouse.

From the other side of the wall, Janice could already hear the first screams.

She stood helplessly. The back exit to the loading dock was completely aflame. There was no way in or out of the expo-center's main hall from this direction.

But she could hear the chaos. Without power, it would be pitch-black.

Except for the fire.

Janice shut her eyes. She could picture the people, panicked and crowding for the exits, falling over each other in the dark.

And the floor at their feet would be *moving*.

Just the smoke right there in the loading dock was almost too thick to breathe. Janice turned for the open bay doors.

But first, she grabbed up her snake-hook and catch-bag, then the first-aid pack from her duffle.

She could see the open pavement outside the bay-door. *At least* a dozen of her donations had made it off the truck. She saw several cobras, including the king.

What had Jack said? *You might need me.*

Janice supposed it didn't matter. They would have carted him off to jail anyway. The city had enabled this disaster to the point of complicity.

With the smoke now becoming asphyxiating, Janice followed the retreating serpents out the bay doors onto the back dock.

Outside, she could hear the shouts and screams from the expo-hall joined by panic and chaos coming from the front parking-lot as well.

Gripping her snake-hook grimly, Janice knew full-well what she was going to find.

CHAPTER 21

The first thing Janice saw outside on the loading dock was Addy Robins and his two friends, lying all in a row, flat on their backs. They had killed themselves just as dead as hell. The truck would have blown-up like the exhaust of a LAWS rocket right in their faces. Three well-earned Darwin Awards collected all at once.

Janice bent briefly over each of them, cooked and burnt. Addy had a surprised look on his face, looking like nothing but an ornery kid, caught with his hand in the cookie-jar.

But as Janice looked back at the burning building and the coiling serpents, even now encroaching in the surrounding corners, she found it hard to feel sorry for him.

He had done all this. No doubt with incitement and encouragement, but now he had answered for it.

Janice wondered how many others would *also* be having to answer for him today. How many might already be injured or dead, and how many still *would* be, just in the bare minutes yet ahead?

Then she heard the sounds of approaching sirens, rising above the shouts and screams.

Gripping her snake-hook and catch-bag, Janice ran around to the front of the building.

But as she turned the corner, she came to an abrupt running-stop. The scene at the front of the expo-center was chaos, from the burning building to the parking-lot and front drive beyond.

The first anchor-point was the main entrance.

As she circled the building, Janice herself was able to avoid the retreating serpents because they were spaced-out on the open back-lot. The front-entrance was a different story.

Leslie Daniels and her news-crew, still reeling from the explosion, now turned their cameras to the main-gate. What followed was recorded live, and broadcast directly to the public.

The front of the expo-center was a two-way entrance/exit, four-doors wide, and normally enough for an orderly procession in and out.

Today, however, with smoke and fire licking at their tails, snakes and humans were competing for the same exits.

The main entranceway quickly bottle-necked and piled-up, as people were knocked down, some trampled, a lot of them shouting and screaming – and a lot of them were being bitten as the very ground at their feet was *moving* – slithering – *writhing* – as the escaping snakes fled the burning building in droves.

And as the clumsy humans were practically running on top of them, these snakes, already fully-aroused, and regardless of species, were *all* biting with full venom-loads.

Janice stood for a moment, agape, helpless to do anything but watch it happen.

She saw the snakes streaming from the building, slipping through the legs of those that managed to escape outside, striking repeatedly as they went, some clinging to people's arms and legs like bulldogs. Their howls and shrieks were matched by the screams of people still trapped inside the Expo, being burned alive.

And now all the escaping vipers and cobras went slithering out into the crowd waiting outside, swarming in the dozens, right into visitor and protester alike.

Janice heard Officers Cates and Hammond, almost simultaneously, “Holy *shit!*”

There was an immediate eruption of gunfire, as they began to pick off the fleeing serpents, even as they washed into the crowd like a tide.

Screams immediately answered the gunfire, even as the wave of snakes hit their feet.

Janice heard Leslie Daniels' voice rise up in a shrill scream.

“Oh my GOD!”

With more agility than Janice would have given her credit for, Leslie, turned and jumped up on top of the news-van, like a squirrel monkey. There was a mutter of cursing, as her crew scrambled-up to join her.

Officers Cates and Hammond glanced at each other before likewise climbing atop their own cruiser, standing on the hood and the roof as they continued to pick off the scattering snakes. Palmer and Baker hadn't moved from their security-van.

It had only been bare minutes, and the fire-department vehicles were just now pulling to a stop.

The fire spread quickly through the roof of the building, which was really mostly all the big open hall was. Except of course, for old Mr. Wilson's office.

Janice wondered if he was still up there when the fire broke out. There was no reason he wouldn't have been. She didn't see him among any of the people that had managed to make their way out.

Neither did she see college-guy Dave, or gypsy Lola, or old Dr. Walton.

That most likely meant they were still inside.

Janice wondered how bad it was. No windows, no lights except for the fire, but full of clouding black smoke – and hundreds of venomous serpents crawling around you in the dark.

Now the fire-department was preparing to run right in, past the crawling menagerie spilling out the front gates.

Janice heard their first shouts of alarm as the fire-team pulled their trucks up beside Officers Cates and Hammond, standing on their cruiser.

"Jesus," the driver shouted out to the others, as the squad hopped out, suited-up, but stepping warily, "what the hell *are* these things?"

"Every goddamn poisonous snake in the friggin' world," Cates hollered back from the top of his car. "There are probably a lot more inside."

Still standing at the corner of the lot, Janice waved her snake-hook for attention, and started forward, but the fire-crew already had a solution.

Quickly hooking up their hoses, they began spraying their way clear.

This washed the swarming serpents away from the main gate, clearing the way for the rescue-crew, but it also had the effect of tossing them into rough, pissed-off clusters to either side, prompting another slithering exodus-rush right into the already panicking crowd.

A whole new multitude of screams erupted as the people scattered like a rack of pool balls.

Leslie Daniels' crew, propped on top of her van, filmed it all.

It would have been near-comedy if wasn't so absolutely deadly.

The crowd of visitors and protesters merged as both groups simply fled in panic on foot, running for the main gates. Brief bursts of screams continued to erupt as one person or another stepped-on, or toppled over an angry cobra or viper.

Janice stood with her hook in her hand, unsure what direction to move first. To her knowledge, there had never been an incident like this anywhere.

Gunshots continued to ring as Hammond and Cates picked targets. Now more police sirens were sounding – more guns on the way.

Meanwhile the fire-crew turned their hoses on the expo-center itself.

There were no more survivors attempting to force their way through the main gates, but the crew was pushing past the piled bodies, forcing their way inside anyway. Their team covered them with hoses trained both on the flames and any malevolent slithering in the corners.

As Janice now made her way to the main lot, she got a better look at the front entrance. One of the bodies piled-up outside was Lola. Her pretty gypsy-face was burnt and her long-hair was singed down to nothing. Janice couldn't tell if that was what killed her.

Most of the escaping serpents were congregating along the main drive, escaping into the open brush that trailed along the through-way leading to the expo-center.

Predictably, most of the instinctive *human* reactions sent them running the other way, although not before both paths crossed in the parking-lot.

Janice couldn't even guess how many people had been bitten already, in just the few minutes since the truck first blew.

Even with the Venom Lab, only a few miles away, they would never have enough antivenin for each species, to treat every bite. Considering the amounts needed to treat even one snakebite-victim, they were going to clean out their entire supply.

Absently, Janice made a mental note to call Venom One in Florida, and get them started on emptying every source in range in the country.

She wielded her snake-hook, feeling ridiculously inadequate, like a knight off to fight an army of dragons with a pair of tongs and a butterfly-sack on a pole.

The pavement was wet and soaked from the fire-hoses. As she approached, coming from the side of the building, the fire-crew shouted unintelligibly over the noise, waving her back – the direction she was going anyway.

There were more ambulances arriving on the scene, pulling up next to the cop cars and fire-trucks.

The crowd had mostly retreated back along the main drive, keeping to the pavement, away from the surrounding brush. Most of the escaping serpents went for the bushes.

Although not all. There were still a few outbursts and screams after someone discovered a cobra or a big lance-head taking refuge under one of the parked cars.

The crowd had already broken into several small groups, where people were attempting to administer care to the injured, who at a glance, Janice already counted in the dozens. Some were burn victims, but most of them were bites.

That meant no real help was coming until she herself actually got into gear, and turned the lights back on at the Institute.

Janice glanced back at the burning building. There were bodies scattered the length of the drive, leading all the way to the pile of corpses, lying half-cooked at the front-door to the expo-center.

The arriving paramedics paused at each of these, making certain, but doing their best to focus their attention on those still alive.

As Janice made her way through the lot, she now saw a couple of bodies she recognized.

Donna Campbell was one. She had been knocked over in her wheelchair, apparently encumbered enough to get tangled-up, and something bit her. Perhaps another cobra. Based on her dead face, Janice would guess an elapid. Something had caused paralysis and shut down her breathing.

That was really the tell-tale difference. Excepting the odd Cascabel or Gaboon adder, most viper-bite victims were the ones moaning in pain. The elapid-bites left you lying very still. It didn't take very long to get dead, after your lungs or heart simply stopped working. And if you were talking your mamba or krait, that didn't take very long at all.

Janice did not see Donna Campbell's son, who had been walking beside her earlier.

The other wheelchair was upright, but empty. Tommy Doyle and his mom had both apparently elected to simply hoof-it on foot.

Janice almost snickered grimly – good for them.

Then she heard a groan.

Leaning with her back against a parked mini-van was Mrs. Janelle Robins. She was holding her leg, which was already swollen and purple.

Facing her, ready to strike again, was a Terciopelo, *Bothrops asper,* commonly called the '*Fer-de-lance*', and the particular species most-often associated with that name, although it was actually a closely-related cousin to the true *B. lanceolatus*.

B. asper was Janice' pick for worst snake to handle, even more than the mambas. They were big, up to seven-feet long, with viper-thickness, and could weigh more than twenty-five pounds. Handling them was like wrestling with a giant muscle, even more than a comparably-sized python, because the constrictor would *wrap* – the viper was *fighting* you, trying to twist just enough in your grip to get those inch-long fangs in you – and then they would *cling* like a bulldog, injecting their entire load.

There was a reason *B. asper* was feared throughout its range.

It looked as if this one had already bitten Mrs. Robins once, and not a dry-bite based on the immediate swelling.

Janice hooked the snake's tail with her tongs, pulling it away from Janelle Robins' still-vulnerable leg. Mrs. Robins shrieked as the snake was yanked out of range, and now circled back towards Janice herself.

This was where these big lance-heads were scary. Once you picked a fight, they would come after you, even more than the mambas.

Janice was *really* wishing Jack was there today.

She had broken into a sweat. She was good with rattlers, but *B. asper* was like a diamondback on crack. They had the same range and speed, but they just *freaked*-out.

All you could do was keep that hook on their tail and keep them folding over themselves.

Then, once you got them moving in a repeating pattern, you offered them the catch-bag, and let them slide right into it.

This particular viper, however, was resisting, and Janice was getting tired. Her grip on the tongs was getting loose.

So instead, she tossed the bag over the writhing snake's back, pressing the pole against its neck.

Moving quickly, she relinquished her grip with tongs on the tail, and reapplied them right behind the neck.

Leaning one knee on the catch-bag, pinning the snake down, she now let the pole loose and grabbed the snake behind the jaws.

She took a moment to catch her breath. These adders were strong. She had to be careful. Moving quickly, she pulled the catch-bag over the pinned viper's head, and tossed the coils in on top. Then she grabbed up the pole, and with her hand still firm on the snake's neck, she stood, letting go her grip and dropping the loose viper inside the bag.

With a twist of the pole, she sealed the top.

Her heart beating, Janice looked down at the captured snake writhing inside the bag.

She almost laughed again, allowing herself a brief moment of self-congratulation. She wished Jack was there again, just to *see* that one.

Janice looked around the lot.

There were a lot of dead snakes to go around now too. There were four cops on site now, the second-pair with scoped rifles, continuing to pick-off one slithering serpent at a time.

Janice allowed herself one pang of regret for the lost lives of all those animals on top of everything else, just over the stupidity of a few dumb-ass humans.

Now she had to worry about saving *all* their lives.

The initial rush of conflict was done. The snakes and people both, typical to their natures, were avoiding each other. Janice saw a number of the vipers still hovering at the edge of the brush, stubbornly holding their ground, especially, all the different lance-heads. Most of the cobras had already vamoosed for the surrounding grasslands.

It was mostly open field on the through-way leading out to Highway 26.

Thirty highly-venomous snakes had been released the night of the break-in at the Institute, and they'd had a checklist to count.

Today, she had absolutely no idea how many might have just been sent swarming into the surrounding acres.

They were within a few short miles of everything from schools, to neighborhoods, to shopping centers, to parks.

Janice shut her eyes, forcing herself calm. That was always the first step in this business.

Mrs. Robins was moaning in pain beneath her. Janice set the catch-bag with the viper in it aside, carefully folding the pole over the top. Then she pulled a pressure-bandage from her first-aid pack.

As Janice bent to examine her bite, Mrs. Robins looked around at the surrounding chaos. Then she stared back balefully at Janice, her eyes full of venom-induced pain.

"What have you *done* here today?" she demanded.

Janice blinked, taken aback.

For a moment, she paused, sitting back, and was nearly tempted to simply step away, to leave this woman here, snake-bit, and deny her treatment.

That's an hour in Purgatory, as Jack would say.

Then Janice remembered Addy. He and his two friends were currently lying dead, just around the corner of the building that they had set on fire.

This woman had just lost her son and didn't even know it yet.

Janice looked down at Mrs. Robins reluctantly. She knew that glowering, sullen hatred would not be dimmed after it was soon cross-fed with angry grief.

For a moment, Janice almost told her. Then she realized it was an angry impulse, which meant it would be cruel.

Instead, she bent to render aid. Because, in the end, that's what she was – a doctor. And even though she was technically more of a chemist, her specialty in venomous snakes *was* really, ultimately, all about saving people's lives.

Ingrate bitch that they might be, Janice thought, glancing down at Janelle Robins.

Almost disliking herself, Janice bent down to help anyway, unwinding the pressure-bandage.

As she did so, something hit her in the shin.

And then again.

It didn't hurt at all.

And *that*, Janice realized, was a *bad* thing.

Peering right next to the tire beside her foot, Janice recognized the retreating form of a common krait.

It had probably actually been zeroing-in on Mrs. Robins. Janice had just kneeled down, and gotten in the way.

She looked down at the four clear puncture marks on her calf – two bites.

"Oh *no*," Janice whispered.

She sat back numbly, and realized she was probably going to die.

CHAPTER 22

Jack was sitting in a holding cell with three other guys – one drunk sleeping it off, one younger guy who looked like a career street-punk, and a DUI arrest, still waiting processing.

As for his own charges, Jack wasn't really sure exactly what they even *were* yet. If somebody in the D.A.'s office was listening to Janelle Robins, it could be anything from manslaughter to negligent homicide.

It was Officer Benton that rapped the cell door, unlocking and opening up.

"Hey, Jack?" he said, poking his head in. "You need to come with us. Right now."

Jack stood, glancing at his cellmates with a shrug.

Officer Jensen was waiting in the hall.

"You're on temporary leave, by order of the town mayor, who also happens to be acting police chief," she said.

Jack had met the mayor, a pure politician, named Wilkins, who had obviously gotten some phone calls. Jack felt a thread of disquiet. The immediacy of his release implied some urgency.

Jensen read out events at the expo-center in deliberately emotionless cop-talk, as the two officers walked him out to their cruiser.

Jack was actually stunned to silence.

"What about Janice?" he said, climbing into the back of the cruiser. "She was working there today."

Officer Jensen's professional tone didn't change. But her eyes flashed a grim glance over her shoulder.

"We don't know," she said. "Dr. McCoy isn't answering her phone."

Jack frowned.

"What about Chuck and Lindsey?"

"We don't have their direct numbers," Jensen said.

Jack looked at his empty pockets. They hadn't even run him through processing. He didn't have his car keys, his wallet, or his phone.

He recited both Chuck and Lindsey's numbers. Jensen dialed both with no response.

"I sent them out snake-hunting in the woods today," Jack said unhappily, although that was less worrisome than Janice, who shouldn't be out of signal-range.

Officer Benton at the wheel squealed tires out of the cop-depot, and wasted little time over the few miles across town to the expo-center.

Jack could see smoke billowing in the sky even before they pulled onto the main drive.

But by now, it was all practically over.

The fire-crew had the burning building doused. The billowing smoke was now mostly clouding steam as the last flames burnt out.

And likewise, most of the escaped serpents that hadn't been shot dead, had already retreated into the surrounding shrubbery.

What Jack saw was mostly the grisly aftermath.

Benton parked the cruiser next to Hammond and Cates, who were caucusing with the other officers, all with guns still drawn, ready to cover the teams of paramedics.

Jensen let Jack out of the back of the cruiser. As he stepped out, his gaze panned slowly from the burnt remains of the expo-center to the human wreckage in its parking-lot.

There were a lot of dead snakes lying around too. But he was going to bet it wasn't anywhere near as many that got away. There wasn't even a way to *begin* to tell what had just been released.

Jack turned, scanning the surrounding fields.

They were less than a mile from the nearest neighborhoods, but there were also miles of woodlands and open fields, until you got to the highway. Then it was farms and forest up into the hills.

Jack looked around helplessly. As near as he could tell, all the damage was already done.

"Honestly," he said, "I don't even know what you want me to *do* here."

Officer Benton looked just as helpless.

"Hell, I don't know. Advise. *Catch* something."

Jack looked around at the curled snake carcasses, and Officers Cates and Hammond, and the other two officers, all still standing ready with their guns. Security-officers Palmer and Baker still hadn't gotten out of their van.

"I think anything that needs catching is already headed for the hills. Right now, we've got people needing help."

Jack indicated the teams of paramedics attending to the injured. They were scattered across the lot, bent over people who were simply lying where they had fallen. At least the medics seemed up-to-date on what they were dealing with. The last few weeks had been prep-training. They had pressure-bandages, and respirators where necessary.

There were also several bodies with sheets thrown over them – too fresh for even the chalk outlines in the pavement.

Among the victims receiving treatment, Jack saw Janelle Robins, propped on a stretcher with an IV in her arm. She was crying, and looked in pain, attended by two medics at once.

It looked like a viper-bite. It probably hurt. But she would probably live. If it was from a Bothrops, they had a lot of antivenin on hand. None of the lance-heads had escaped the Institute, so none of their on-hand supply had been needed.

Then Jack heard his name – a ghost-whisper, amplified by mechanical breathing.

On a stretcher being loaded onto the nearest ambulance, was Janice.

A nurse hovered above her, helping her breathe with a respirator, and her attempt to speak was a guttural spasm. The nurse was looking up at Jack grimly.

"Her symptoms came on fast," the nurse said. "First general paralysis. Then she started having trouble breathing. But when she could still talk, she said it was a common krait bite."

Jack shut his eyes. This nurse didn't know what that meant.

But Janice did. Jack could tell by the look in her eye, even though she couldn't move.

Jack leaned beside the stretcher, taking her hand. A single tear blinked out of her eye, even as the respirator forced her breath in and out.

A common krait bite was fatal fifty-percent of the time, even with antivenin treatment, and the reason was because the paralysis it caused was irreversible.

Janice was already on the respirator, unable to breathe on her own.

It was a severe envenomation. Her respiratory system was already shutting down. For all practical purposes, antivenin was too late.

Janice was going to die. Right now, right in front of him.

The last conversation he'd had with her played in his head. She'd laughed about the *'jump-your-bones-McCoy'* thing, and told him he was a pretty good kisser.

Now she was looking up at him, blinking tears and scared, unable to talk, or even move.

Jack held her limp, boneless hand, not knowing what else to do, but to just be *there* – smiling gently, deliberately not crying himself, whispering, telling her not to be afraid.

More tears blinked from her eyes.

Jack felt her hand squeeze his, a last muscular spasm.

And then she was gone.

The respirator-unit continued to pump, forcing her chest robotically up and down, but the nurse looked at Jack solemnly and nodded, shutting it off.

Jack's eyes squeezed shut.

Pain would come later. Right now, it felt a lot like being hit with a stunning physical blow, that left you momentarily numb.

He looked up at Officers Benton and Jensen, who both looked a little teary themselves.

"Jack," Benton said, helplessly, "I sure am sorry. But we still need your help."

Jack clutched Janice' still-warm hand.

That threatened the numbness.

Time to go cold, he thought. For the immediate future.

"Yeah," he replied to Benton. "Yeah, you do."

Janice wore her key-chain on her belt, along with her university ID. Feeling a bit ghoulish, Jack unclipped both.

He gave her hand a last squeeze. But it was empty clay. She wasn't there anymore.

Jack stood, looking out at the terrain beyond the expo-center parking lot. It was halfway between downtown and the highway, roughly the same distance to all the same neighborhoods as the Institute, just coming from the west, with all the same brush and woodlands.

At least hundreds of snakes and reptiles had just been released into those open fields. Most of them were venomous, and all of them were invasive.

Jack turned to Officer Benton.

"Clear everyone out of here, and get them to the hospital. Right now."

"What about all those loose snakes?" Benton asked.

"Not a priority. You're going to need a whole team to deal with that. Experienced snake-catchers." He nodded over to Hammond and Cates. "You're never going to be able to shoot them all. Get on the news and tell people in the surrounding neighborhoods to be on their highest alert."

Jack held up Janice' keys, hitting the beeper, and a horn started blinking where she'd parked at the back of the lot near the exit. Jack started walking towards it.

"Wait a minute," Benton said. "Where do you think you're going? You're technically still in custody."

Jack kept walking.

"I'm going to the Institute," he said, over his shoulder. "The hospital is going to need antivenin in large quantities for multiple species. With Janice gone, I'm the only one with the authority or the code to get in. I'm also going to need to get Venom One on the horn, and get them hunting down more local sources for us. Because we're going to run out fast. Meanwhile, I'll start inventorying what we've got on hand, and start rousting every toxicology specialist for a hundred miles."

Benton and Jensen looked indecisive.

"Jack..." Benton began.

Jack stopped, looking back, pointing to Janice, still on her stretcher at the back of the ambulance, although the nurse had covered her up.

"Fifteen minutes was the difference for my friend over there under that sheet," he said. "Every minute you bullshit me is the difference for somebody here that's still alive."

Benton started forward.

"I'll drive you..." he began, but Jack cut him off.

"Stay and help here. You know where I am. You still have my damn phone, house keys, and my wallet. If the city fathers want to put me back in jail after this, you can come find me."

Benton sighed, glancing at Jensen who nodded.

"His arrest was bullshit, anyway," she agreed.

Jack nodded, turning back, spotting Janice' little eco-rig. He glanced down at the keys in his hand. They were attached to her ID-photo, smiling, and every bit as unflattering as a driver's license picture.

She was still a pretty woman, though. And a pretty good kisser.

As of two minutes ago, she was a cooling cadaver.

When he got into her car, it smelled like her perfume. He saw her *Heart-Coffee* mug, and when he started the engine, the radio was tuned to that easy-listening station she liked.

These were all daggers, threatening the numbness.

With a physical effort, he summoned back the cold, even as his foot clenched involuntarily on the gas, squealing the tires past the emergency vehicles, as he squirreled out of the parking-lot.

CHAPTER 23

As Jack slid Janice' little eco-wagon silently into the Institute parking-lot, it took him a moment to figure out what was wrong.

The lights were out. The power was off.

There was no stormy weather, and the surrounding block seemed to be working fine. It was just inside the lot.

A light thread of disquiet twanged his heart like a guitar-string when he saw Lindsey's car, that gas-guzzling sixties Mustang, parked right up near the entrance.

Neither Lindsey or Chuck had answered when Officer Benton had tried to call.

Jack parked next to the old Mustang. On inspection, the car was empty.

But now as he looked towards the main building, he saw that the door to the employee-entrance had been jimmied.

Jack frowned.

That thread of disquiet was now a full-chord.

Cautiously, he approached, keeping his eye out for the slithering movement of anything that might have been let loose all over again.

For a moment, Jack paused. He might be better advised to call the police before venturing in alone. Except he had no phone.

Jack glanced back at Lindsey's empty car before pushing open the broken door and venturing into the darkened Institute.

It was daytime, but there were no windows inside. The solar roof-panels filtered a certain amount of light, dimly illuminating the main hallways.

But it was still quite dark. Jack wished he had a flashlight. He tried to keep to the center of the hall, away from dark corners, as he crept warily towards the Venom Lab.

And as he approached, there was enough light to see the broken glass on the floor, where the door to the lab had been kicked in.

Jack was beginning to wish he had something in his hands – a snake-hook – or a club.

He wondered who might be waiting in there. Or what might be crawling around loose.

In the dark.

He thought of Lindsey's car outside. Then he thought of Janice.

Setting his teeth, Jack pushed open the broken, hanging door.

The first thing he saw when he stepped inside was a body lying on the floor.

For one terrified moment, Jack thought it might be Lindsey. But then in the dim light, he saw it was a man, dressed in shabby camouflage, with a mop of unkempt dark hair and a beard.

As Jack bent over him, he realized that this was James Warden – *the Warden,* self-styled justice-warrior – now deceased.

This was actually the first time Jack had ever seen him in person.

Nice to meet ya, you son of a bitch.

Even in the dark, Jack recognized signs of suffocation from respiratory paralysis.

The fact that James Warden was lying on the floor meant he hadn't moved far after the bite. That meant it had dropped him fast.

That would imply the black mamba.

Jack glanced around in the shadowed light, peering into each corner, straining to see in the half-dark.

Then, from just inside the main lab, where all the most toxic herps were contained, he heard the ever-so-slightest whimper, an abbreviated breath.

A moment later, a curt whispered command: "*Shut up!*"

Jack stood, stepping over James Warden on the floor. He pushed open the door to the lab.

Lindsey was in there, standing next to the mamba-cage.

So was Chuck. He had his arm wrapped around her neck, propping her in front of him.

In his other hand, he was holding a gun to her head.

CHAPTER 24

The top of the mamba-cage was ajar. The snake sat inside, coiled and agitated, displaying with its open ebony-black mouth.

Jack made the educated guess it was James Warden who lifted the cage-lid. Jack further guessed it had been at gunpoint.

In the dim-light, he could see Lindsey crying silently.

"Chuck?" Jack said incredulously. "What's going on?"

Inside the cage, the mamba's head poked briefly at the open top. Jack made an instinctive move to stop it, but the gun at Lindsey's head turned in his direction.

"Don't move, Jack," Chuck said.

Jack stopped. Fortunately, so did the mamba, resting its head along the cage top, protruding barely six-inches beyond the glass.

Lindsey blinked, streaming silent tears, as Chuck held her near the cage. She kept rigidly still, her eyes locked on the agitated serpent, but Jack could see the involuntary shudder, knowing her personal dread. Lindsey was always a bit phobic about the mambas.

The snake reared-up another ten-inches or so, eyeing the two odd house apes that seemed to pester it.

"Lindsey?" Jack said. "Are you okay?"

She nodded, but her voice was choked.

"Jack," she said, "I think he killed Brad. I think he did *all* of this..."

But Chuck jerked his hand over her mouth.

"I said *shut-up!*"

Jack poised, ready to move, but the gun remained aimed unerringly right at him. He glanced back at

James Warden's prone form, then back at Chuck. At least they could stop wondering who gave the security code to Liz Williams and her friends the night of the break-in.

Chuck's eyes were wide. At twenty-three, he still looked like the wide-eyed, naive kid Jack met at sixteen.

But the look there now was sly, more like the teen-delinquent who'd been having it over on his clueless, trusting parents for a long time, but was now found out.

"Chuck?" Jack asked again. "What are you doing here?"

But even as he asked the question, he knew. All it took was for the events of the last few weeks to flash sequentially past his recollection, and understanding dawned.

It was the power-outage – that was the tell. Last time, it had been in the hours before the break-in, a period when the security cameras were off, and then conveniently clicked back on so the doors with security codes could operate.

The outage that night hadn't been the weather. Just like it wasn't tonight. The security cameras needed to be off, to hide specific details best kept off the record.

Chuck eyed Jack nervously, with those same caught-kid eyes.

"It was *you*," Jack said, "that took the mamba that night. *Before* the break-in. Before Liz Williams and her friends even got there."

The vandals needed a code for an operating security lock, which wouldn't have worked with the lights out. But Jack himself made certain all his employees had keys to the fire door. For safety.

He was nodding to himself, involuntarily. It was like a kinked-joint popping loose, releasing a numbness he wasn't even aware of. A situation he thought he fully understood was suddenly cast in a totally new light –

like one of those 3D pictures that becomes a completely different image if you adjust your focus.

In this case, if you disregarded the ever-so carefully crafted appearance of random circumstance and looked for a guiding hand.

Like say, a fall-guy keeping score.

Jack remembered joking about the teenage psycho-revenge movies – the angry nerds and their grudges over prom-night.

And of course, every psycho needed a trigger, something to focus every real and perceived slight – like getting punched out in a cafe, or hit with a skateboard, or getting your internship blocked – or even something so simple as getting royally and publicly knocked on your ass by the prom queen at a frat party.

Of course, that would assume a fairly advanced psychosis. Those things didn't just happen. They developed over time, often starting from trauma in childhood.

Like your brother dying from a rattlesnake bite.

That would have certainly been traumatic. Jack could testify it was when it happened to him.

But now he found himself wondering if in Chuck's case, it was really more about leading your brother to a pre-scouted rattlesnake-nest to make camp for the night?

What had Chuck said? His brother used to take after him something awful?

And now for some reason, here was Lindsey too. Jack wondered if she'd caught on to him somehow.

Or perhaps, Chuck had discovered that, even with Bradley Brown gone, Lindsey still didn't want him.

All this supposition flashed through Jack's head in bare instants, while the three of them stood at an indecisive tableau.

Still propped-up, barely out of its cage, the mamba seemed to regard them curiously, perhaps recognizing the tension was not aimed in its direction, but still ready to strike at a moment. Jack had seen mambas pose this way as herds of buffalo would pass, the wary beasts giving the snake a dutiful space.

Chuck glanced warily at the mamba, maintaining his distance, keeping Lindsey between them.

Jack's eyes narrowed. The cold-bloodedness was undeniable. He'd known Chuck a lot of years, and he found it hard to accept, even at face-value.

For just a moment, it seemed possible to reach out to the human.

“Chuck?” Jack asked, almost wonderingly. “Did you really *do* this?”

Chuck's nervous glare faltered briefly.

“Dammit, Jack,” he said regretfully. “Why'd you have to show up here tonight?”

“Let her go, Chuck. How many people are dead already?”

Now the sly-kid looked flustered – a kid who perhaps lit a bigger fire than he intended.

“This wasn't supposed to go any further than the break-in that night.”

Chuck shook his head, eyeing Jack defiantly, frustrated.

“I let the other mamba loose. And the taipan, and a couple of cobras. I figured once they kicked over that little chemical-in-a-bucket firetrap I set for them, that would be enough.”

Jack nodded noncommittally, as Chuck confessed to deliberate murder. You usually didn't do that to someone you had at gunpoint, who you intended to let live.

“I didn't really expect,” Chuck said, “for those idiots to let everything else out of their cages.”

And now, Chuck shrugged.

For Jack, that shrug brought it all home.

It was... callous.

The damage was done. This was the kid trying to cover his tracks from the burned-down barn.

Jack nodded to James Warden, lying cooling behind them.

"So why is *he* here? Just a patsy?"

Chuck shrugged again.

"A semi-useful idiot. I told him I had evidence that would prove his innocence and hang the Institute at the same time."

"And dead patsies don't talk," Jack remarked.

Chuck frowned.

"His people punched my face in. Cracked my head with a goddamn skateboard."

Chuck rubbed his nose, which was swollen, and gave Lindsey a smart shake.

"I don't like getting *hit*," Chuck scowled, purposefully.

Jack regarded Chuck musingly. Kind of a little-man's syndrome, he thought. His own approach to bullies had been to take karate.

Upon quick reflection, Jack decided he didn't really have as much in common with Chuck as he thought.

Although the kid had apparently been ready to show due respect for his mentor.

"I wasn't going to include you," Chuck said. "They would have just found them both. The broken door and the loose snake would sell it."

Found them both.

Jack recognized the immediate significance of that phrasing.

Lindsey obviously did as well. Her eyes were locked on the mamba cage, whose occupant remained perched, its head poking just over the top, hovering in a cobra-pose not four-feet away.

It could move in a second. At over ten-feet long, it

could come over the top of its tank in the blink of an eye.

Jack could hear his own pulse in his head, as he met Lindsey's terrified eyes, as she was propped up like a helpless human shield, between him and the kid who he'd projected so much of himself into – the same pretty girl, the same jock boyfriend.

Except, when Jack had gotten his heart broken and his ass kicked, he had simply walked away, bloody nose, bruises and all.

Was that all this was about? Getting hit?

Brad? Janice? Liz Williams? Even James Warden?

Jack met Chuck's eye levelly. He knew what he had to do.

"Let her go," Jack said. "It's not too late. Not for her."

Chuck half-smirked, before his face grew stony.

"Yeah. Yeah, it is."

Chuck pushed Lindsey forwards towards the mamba-cage. The gun at her head forgotten, Lindsey instinctively started to struggle.

In the cage, the mamba moved in a flash – the slippery whiplash of a spider-strand, the black mouth darting wide-open at the threatening movement.

But Jack was there first, stepping his body between Lindsey and the mamba's strike.

The first bite caught him in the shoulder, the second in the stomach. And as he grabbed the thrashing snake like a wild, squirting hose, he caught two more, one in each hand, before catching the mamba firmly behind the head.

Jack's head went light almost immediately, as the venom coursed through his bloodstream like a highball.

He heard Lindsey scream.

She was struggling for the pistol. Chuck was just prying away Lindsey's grasping fingers, and pushing her away, as Jack caught Chuck's gun-hand firmly by the wrist.

With his other hand, Jack pressed the struggling mamba's head right into Chuck's throat.

The mamba obliged readily enough, sinking its fangs precisely as Jack intended – straight into the jugular, injecting its full venom-load.

Chuck screamed.

Now, Jack wrested the gun away. In an instant, he pivoted, swinging the pistol butt-first, just as hard as he could, directly into Chuck's temple.

The kid went down, limp and unconscious. With the mamba venom coursing through him, he wouldn't live long enough to wake.

Moving quickly, Jack turned, dragging the mamba back and shoving it bodily inside the cage, popping the top solidly back on. The snake thrashed and coiled inside.

And Jack dropped to the floor.

He felt the cold tile hit his face. He saw Chuck's still form lying on the white antiseptic tile.

Then Jack felt Lindsey's arms upon him. He looked up and could see but not hear as she called his name.

He was able to smile at her, just a little.

Then there was a sense of falling.

And then the world went black.

THE END

Check out other great

Cryptid Novels!

P.K. Hawkins

THE CRYPTID FILES

Fresh out of the academy with top marks, Agent Bradley Tennyson is expecting to have the pick of cases and investigations throughout the country. So he's shocked when instead he is assigned as the new partner to "The Crag," an agent well past his prime. He thinks the assignment is a punishment. It's anything but.Agent George Crag has been doing this job for far longer than most, and he knows what skeletons his bosses have in the closet and where the bodies are buried. He has pretty much free reign to pick his cases, and he knows exactly which one he wants to use to break in his new young partner: the disappearance and murder of a couple of college kids in a remote mountain town.Tennyson doesn't realize it, but Crag is about to introduce him to a world he never believed existed: The Cryptid Files, a world of strange monsters roaming in the night. Because these murders have been going on for a long time, and evidence is mounting that the murderer may just in fact be the legendary Bigfoot.

Gerry Griffiths

DOWN FROM BEAST MOUNTAIN

A beast with a grudge has come down from the mountain to terrorize the townsfolk of Porterville. The once sleepy town is suddenly wide awake. Sheriff Abel McGuire and game warden Grant Tanner frantically investigate one brutal slaying after another as they follow the blood trail they hope will eventually lead to the monstrous killer. But they better hurry and stop the carnage before the census taker has to come out and change the population sign on the edge of town to ZERO.

Check out other great

Cryptid Novels!

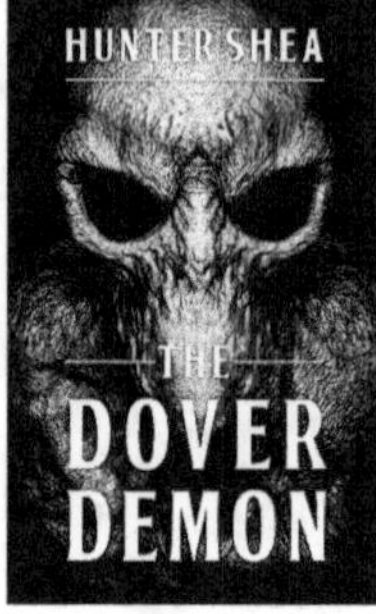

Hunter Shea

THE DOVER DEMON

The Dover Demon is real...and it has returned. In 1977, Sam Brogna and his friends came upon a terrifying, alien creature on a deserted country road. What they witnessed was so bizarre, so chilling, they swore their silence. But their lives were changed forever. Decades later, the town of Dover has been hit by a massive blizzard. Sam's son, Nicky, is drawn to search for the infamous cryptid, only to disappear into the bowels of a secret underground lair. The Dover Demon is far deadlier than anyone could have believed. And there are many of them. Can Sam and his reunited friends rescue Nicky and battle a race of creatures so powerful, so sinister, that history itself has been shaped by their secretive presence? "THE DOVER DEMON is Shea's most delightful and insidiously terrifying monster yet." – Shotgun Logic Reviews "An excellent horror novel and a strong standout in the UFO and cryptid subgenres." –Hellnotes "Non-stop action awaits those brave enough to dive into the small town of Dover, and if you're lucky, you won't see the Demon himself!" – The Scary Reviews PRAISE FOR SWAMP MONSTER MASSACRE "B-horror movie fans rejoice, Hunter Shea is here to bring you the ultimate tale of terror!" – Horror Novel Reviews "A nonstop thrill ride! I couldn't put this book down." – Cedar Hollow Horror Reviews

Armand Rosamilia

THE BEAST

The end of summer, 1986. With only a few days left until the new school year, twins Jeremy and Jack Schaffer are on very different paths. Jeremy is the geek, playing Dungeons & Dragons with friends Kathleen and Randy, while Jack is the jock, getting into trouble with his buddies. And then everything changes when neighbor Mister Higgins is killed by a wild animal in his yard. Was it a bear? There's something big lurking in the woods behind their New Jersey home.Will the police be able to solve the murder before more Middletown residents are ripped apart?

www.ingramcontent.com/pod-product-compliance
Lightning Source LLC
Chambersburg PA
CBHW061243170626
46809CB00007B/2798

* 9 7 8 1 9 2 3 1 6 5 4 7 2 *